FOLK TALES FROM THE FAR EAST

FOLK TALES FROM THE FAR EAST

BY

Charles H. Meeker

Illustrated by

Frederick Richardson

PILGRIMS PUBLISHING

◆ Varanasi ◆

FOLK TALES FROM THE FAR EAST
by **CHARLES H. MEEKER**

Published by:
PILGRIMS PUBLISHING

An imprint of:
PILGRIMS BOOK HOUSE
(Distributors in India)
B 27/98 A-8, Nawabganj Road
Durga Kund, Varanasi-221010, India
Tel: 91-542-2314059, 2314060, 2312456
Fax: 91-542-2312788, 2311612
E-mail: pilgrims@satyam.net.in
Website: www.pilgrimsbooks.com

PILGRIMS BOOK HOUSE (New Delhi)
9 Netaji Subhash Marg, 2nd Floor
Near Neeru Hotel,
Daryaganj,
New Delhi 110002
Tel: 91-11-23285081
E-mail: pilgrim@del2.vsnl.net.in

Distributed in Nepal by:
PILGRIMS BOOK HOUSE
P O Box 3872, Thamel,
Kathmandu, Nepal
Tel: 977-1-4424942
Fax: 977-1-4424943
E-mail: pilgrims@wlink.com.np

First Edition 1927, The John C. Winston Company

ISBN: 81-7769-117-1
Rs.

Layout by Asha
Cover design by Sasya
Illustrations by Frederick Richardson
Edited by Bob Gibbons and Sian Pritchard-Jones with Christopher N Burchett

Printed in India

To my little daughter

MARY JANE

CONTENTS

FOREWORD

Some time ago, I was sitting in the shade of an ancient banyan tree, reading a book of old, old tales. It so happened at the time that I was the only person under the tree, or even near it.

Suddenly a door opened from the side of the great trunk, and a beautiful wood fairy came out. She smiled, then saluted me with the title *Sahib,* a term of respect used by Hindus in addressing Europeans.

"Sahib," began the fairy, "I see you like stories. Do you like riddles, too?"

"Quite well," I said. "A blind Tagal in Manila once taught me several; but that was a long time ago."

"If you can guess my riddle, I shall tell you some stories that have never been written down by man. They have been told thousands and thousands of times, and have always delighted those who listened to them."

"You are very kind,' I acknowledged. "Please give me the riddle; but I hope it will not be difficult, for I would like very much to hear your stories."

Then the fairy gave me this riddle:

"A thousand years ago a tiny prince was stolen by a night prowler, who carried him far away and left him with a woman of a different race. The woman treated the baby kindly, feeding him and watching over him tenderly. When the prince became a young man, he loved his foster mother so much that he smothered her with caresses. He is now adored by creatures of both land and air, for they say he provides a heaven for chattering monkeys; a love bower for gaily colored birds; a conservatory for all fiddling insects; a resting place for weary men, and a paradise for little children. He is the king that never dies."

"Your riddle, O fairy," I said, "is more than a riddle; it is a story. I venture this interpretation of it: -

"The tiny prince was a seed of the Banyan fig; the night prowler was a flying fox that stole the fruit; the woman was a tree unlike the Banyan; the seed took root in the bark of the tree where the animal left it, and was fed by its sap; as the Banyan grew older it wrapped itself about its host, causing it to perish, but not until its own roots had reached the ground. Insects, birds, beasts, and men love the Banyan because it gives them happiness. The Banyan is king of the forest, because it is the largest and most majestic of trees. It never dies, because it keeps sending down prop roots from its heavy branches, and these roots, taking hold in the earth, become new trunks; thus the body is renewed from time to time."

"You are right, Sahib," said the fairy.

So she told me the delightful tales that are found in this book. I hope that you will enjoy them as I did when they were told to me.

THE MISER AND THE BANYAN TREE

In a botanical garden at the edge of a large city in India stands an ancient banyan tree. Its middle body, as big as a house, is surrounded by hundreds of long, twisted prop roots that grow down from wide, heavy branches, and the whole is roofed over with an immense leafy dome. The forest of root columns, the huge, central body, and the mountain of thick, glossy leaves give to the tree such grandeur that travelers sometimes come halfway around the world to see it.

Two or three hundred years ago, the land upon which the majestic tree grows belonged to a rich jute planter called Goldfinger. Although Goldfinger had more money than an elephant could carry, he was such an old miser that he clothed his wife and children in rags, and bought them nothing to eat except musty rice and the cheapest of little dried fishes. He cheated his servants, abused the tax collectors, and had never been known to give so much as a hammered penny toward helping the poor.

One day the jute planter called his servants and said to them: "That ugly tree is spoiling nearly an acre of my good land. Chop it down and dig up its roots. I can then plant the land in jute, and sell the fiber to be made into grain bags."

So the men gathered up their tools and started to work. But as they reached the tree, thousands of birds were singing in its branches; chattering monkeys leaped from limb to limb; children were playing hide and seek among its roots, and in its shade rested many weary travelers.

When the men saw all this they did not have the heart to chop the tree down. They returned to their master, and said: "Sir, it would be a pity to destroy the banyan tree. It is a thing of great beauty, which gives pleasure to birds, beasts, and men. Have you not other land upon which to plant jute? "

Upon hearing these words, Goldfinger was very angry. He snatched the tools from their hands, and walked away muttering that he would destroy the tree himself. Arriving at the tree, he found an old beggar sitting in its shade with his back against one of the wooden bowls, and over his shoulder hung a dingy jute bag. The old man rose and held out his bowl.

"Give me some paisa, please," he begged.

"Begone!" said the miser, "I never give to beggars."

The feeble old man hobbled away, while Goldfinger went back among the columns of roots. When he came to the main trunk he gave it a hard blow with his axe. As he drew back to give a second stroke to his amazement a door suddenly opened in the great trunk, and a beautiful fairy appeared before him.

"Did you knock, sir?" she asked in a friendly voice.

"N-o!" stammered the jute planter, "I was just beginning to chop."

"Come in," said the fairy, not giving him time to finish what he had started to say. "It is our king's birthday, and we are having a feast. You are welcome to enjoy it with us."

"Will it cost me anything?" asked the stingy fellow.

"Oh, no," answered the fairy. "You shall be our guest of honor."

"I might as well enjoy a good meal, as it will cost me nothing," thought the miser. " I shall then have more strength to work."

He followed the fairy into a great hall, which was filled with a light brighter than if the sun were shining into it. In the middle of the hall stood a long table upon which were set hundreds of golden dishes filled with the finest of foods. At the table sat the king, with the lords and ladies of his court, his golden crown upon his head and his jeweled wand at his side. The king, as well as the other fairies, arose to greet their guest; then motioned him to be seated with them.

At first the bright light of the hall and the glitter of so much gold dazzled Goldfinger's eyes. However, after he had become accustomed to the sights, he fell to eating with all his might, gobbling up the food as fast as half a dozen servants could bring it to him.

When the feast was over, the king called Goldfinger aside and asked him how much he would take for the banyan tree and the acre of ground upon which it grew.

"I hadn't thought of selling any of my property," said he, somewhat astonished.

"Is a thousand pieces of gold enough?" asked the fairy king, while his treasurer laid the money upon the table.

"I think I should have two thousand," said the greedy man, eyeing the golden heap. "You know the land is valuable, and the tree is worth much to me in the way of firewood."

"Very well," said the king, laying before him a deed. "Please sign your name to this paper, and the money is yours."

Goldfinger wrote his name upon the paper; then hastily wrapped the money in a coarse handkerchief and placed it inside his coat. As he was putting the money away, the little servants who had waited upon him brought a large basket of food.

"Take this," they said, "to your wife and children, and give them our best wishes."

The jute planter walked outside without even thanking the fairies for the feast he had enjoyed. Sitting down among the roots of the tree he counted the money several times, chuckling over the bargain he had made. When he had finished counting every piece he looked at the basket of food.

"I shall surely not give these good things to that woman and those children of mine," he said to himself. "It would spoil their taste for moldy rice and stale fish." So saying, he began to eat and soon had eaten every bit of the food himself, not even tossing a crumb to the monkeys and the birds, which begged for a portion of it.

After he had eaten the last mouthful he counted his money again. Then he sat thinking and blinking his eyes.

Suddenly he rose, walked back to the door, opened it softly, and looked in. The table and the golden dishes were still there, just as he had left them; but all the fairies except the king were gone. He was still sitting at the table, his golden crown upon his head and his jeweled wand at his side; but he was sound asleep.

"Oho!" chuckled the miser to himself; "the tree is mine; so all that is in it is mine. The money that the elf king paid me is really in the way of rent. What right had he and his people to live in my property all these years unknown to me? I have not been paid enough."

He slipped into the hall. Going to the table, he placed his money in the middle, drew up the corners of the rich cloth, tied them securely over the money and golden dishes, threw the heavy bundle over his shoulder, and started out. As he was leaving, his large, yellow eyes fell upon the sleeping king. He stole over to his side, took off the crown, and picked up the wand. Then taking care to make no noise, he crept out of the hall, through the door into the sunshine.

Once outside again Goldfinger felt a deep sleep coming upon him. He sank down in a shady nook among the roots and soon fell into a deep sleep.

When he awoke, he rubbed his eyes and walked out upon the grounds that surrounded the tree. There he saw thousands of happy people walking about in a great park. Gardeners were busy mowing the soft grass and tending beds of flowers; and children were enjoying themselves in swings that hung from the branches of the tree.

Soon an officer came by and Goldfinger asked: "What does all this mean? Do these trespassers not know that this land is mine? Tell them to be gone!"

"Grandfather," replied the officer kindly, as he looked Goldfinger in the face, "this is a public park. A legend says that the land once belonged to an old miser by the name of Goldfinger, but he went away more than a hundred years ago and was never heard of again. His family later on gave this land and the banyan tree to the city to be made into a park. May I help you in any way?"

"You may help by driving these beggars off my property! " snarled the old miser. " And another thing, stop talking nonsense." The officer walked away with a shake of his head.

In a rage Goldfinger tried to drive the people off himself, but his voice was so weak that it could scarcely be heard a few feet away. His legs, too, felt strangely stiff. "I have caught cold," he thought. "I have slept too long." He sat down upon a bench and looked into the cloth to see if his gold was still there, fearing that he might have been robbed while he slept.

To his horror the silken cloth had turned into an old jute bag, and in it were only a few crusts of stale and broken bread. The golden crown he had stolen from the fairy king's head had become a beggar's bowl and the jeweled wand a crooked staff.

By the aid of the staff Goldfinger hobbled away, the wooden bowl in his hand and the bag over his shoulder. A little child seeing him came up and dropped a penny into the bowl. The miser had become a beggar, like the old man he had driven away when he had come to destroy the banyan tree.

MR. MONK AND MRS. GRAYCAT

Mrs. Graycat and her six kittens were moving to a place on the other side of the mountain. About noon they stopped to rest near a spring. While they were resting, Mr. Monk came to the spring for a cool drink.

"Good morning, Mrs. Graycat," said the monkey.

"Good morning, Mr. Monk," said Mrs. Graycat.

"Good morning, kittens," said the monkey to the kittens.

"Good morning, Mr. Monk," said all the six kittens together.

After the monkey had taken a drink from the spring, Mrs. Graycat asked, "Will you please tell us how long it will take to get to the other side of the mountain?"

The monkey looked for a while at each of the six kittens. "I cannot tell until I know how fast you will go," said he. Then he tried to look very wise. "If you go slowly, you will get there this evening; if you go fast, you will get there tomorrow; but if you go very fast, you will get there next week."

He then made a low bow, said goodbye, and went away.

He had been gone but a short time when Mrs. Graycat said to her kittens: "Come along, children, let us be going. The monkey said we would have to hurry if we wished to reach the other side of the mountain this evening."

"Oh, no, Mother," said the kittens, "that was not what the monkey told you. He said if we traveled slowly, we would reach our new home this evening."

"Nonsense, you foolish kittens!" replied Mrs. Graycat, "anyone ought to know better than that."

"Please, Mother, let us rest a little while longer," said a little wee kitten. "My legs are so tired."

"Come along, you lazy kittens," growled Mrs. Graycat.

So the cat and her six kittens started to run as fast as they could, for the old cat was anxious to reach her new home before sundown.

They had not gone far when the little wee kitten said: "Mother, my feet are so tired. Let us not go so fast."

In a little while one of the other kittens said his feet were tired, too. Then all the other kittens began to complain. So they all fell behind. But the mother cat did not miss them until she was a long way ahead.

"Look, children," she said when she had come to a high place in the road, "just a mile away is our new home."

When she looked around not a kitten was in sight.

"Oh, my dear little kittens!" she mewed. "I thought they were right here with me."

Mrs. Graycat hurried back over the road. Soon she met the strongest kitten, walking along slowly and mewing sadly.

"Where are your brothers and sisters?" she asked.

"I do not know," replied the kitten. "I went so fast that they could not keep up with me."

"Wait here until I find the other kittens," said Mrs. Graycat.

About a mile farther back she found the second strongest kitten, crawling along so slowly that she could hardly tell whether he moved or not. She laid him down at the side of the road and went to look for the other kittens. She found them all along the road, about a mile apart. The little wee kitten was lying in the grass not far from the spring. He was so weak that he could not walk a step.

Mrs. Graycat picked up the little wee kitten in her mouth, and carried him back to where the strongest kitten was. She had to bring all the others, one at a time, in the same way that she had carried the little wee kitten. This work made her very tired, and though she needed rest, she had to stay up most of that night looking after her children.

In the morning five of the kittens cried for something to eat. But the little one was so ill that he was not hungry. Mrs. Graycat had to run all over the woods to find food for the hungry kittens. All she could find were some big grasshoppers. The kittens did not like grasshoppers, but they were so hungry that they ate all their mother brought, and cried for more. Next day she found a nice young mouse. She gave this to the little wee kitten. The others had to eat plain black bugs for their supper.

The little wee kitten was so ill at the end of the fourth day that Mrs. Graycat had to go back to her old home for some catnip. After this the kitten began to get better, and on the morning of the sixth day the cat and her family could go on again.

This time they walked very slowly, but even at that, Mrs. Graycat had to carry the little wee kitten a great part of the way. When they got to their new home, it was just a week from the time they had left the spring, which proves that Mr. Monk knew what he was talking about.

MAGANDA AND THE BANYAN FAIRIES

Maganda was a pretty little orphan, who lived with her uncle and aunt in a small house by the side of the sea. Her uncle and aunt were very poor. Though they were young and strong, they were often sad because they had such a hard time. They sometimes wished that a kind fairy would give them some of the good things which their neighbors enjoyed.

Every afternoon Maganda went into the forest nearby to gather wood for the fire. One evening she had picked up a lot of straight sticks. These she bound into a bundle which she placed upon her head, and then she started home.

Suddenly, the whole forest seemed to be filled with the sweetest music she had ever heard. Stopping to listen, she found that the music came from a huge banyan tree that sent its roots down from its great branches until it covered almost half an acre of ground.

Maganda slipped up very softly to the side of the tree, where she found a door opening into the trunk. Peeping in, she saw a great many fairies, all dressed in the prettiest clothes. They were dancing to strange, beautiful music of guitars, violins, flutes, and other instruments.

Among the musicians there was a little fellow who played a great bass violin, several times larger than himself. Every time he drew the bow back and forth across the strings, the bass violin seemed to say:

"Time flies,
Time dies."

Maganda set her bundle of wood down near the tree and put her head inside the door. In the middle of the room she saw a long table covered with rich cloth, upon which were spread golden dishes filled with the finest foods.

"How nice it would be," thought the little girl, "if I could go in for a few moments. Surely," she said to herself, "the fairies will not hurt me. They are so beautiful and happy."

One of the little men fairies danced near the door. Upon seeing Maganda, he made the most graceful bow that a fairy could possibly make, and invited her into the great hall of the banyan tree. She went in and sat down, and listened to the sweet music and watched the joyful dancing.

Finally, the fairies gathered around the table for the feast. Maganda was given a seat among them as an honored guest, while servants waited upon her as if she had been a princess.

When the banquet was over, the music and the dancing began again. The music was so gay that it seemed to bewitch Maganda, and she could not keep from dancing. She looked at herself as she danced, and she, too, seemed to be a fairy, with the prettiest shoes, and a dress so fine that it might have been woven from spiders' webs.

After the dancing had gone on for some time, Maganda suddenly remembered her uncle and aunt at home. "What will they think? It is already growing dark, and I have been gone almost an hour," she thought.

The little man was still playing the bass violin and the violin still seemed to say:

"Time flies,
Time dies."

She hastily asked if she might leave. Before she went, the little man fairy who had invited her to the dance, gave her a daintily carved casket bound in gold.

"Take this," he said, "for yourself and your good people."

Once outside, Maganda saw that her clothes were the same as she had worn before she entered the home of the fairies. She quickly picked up the bundle of wood, placed it again upon her

Upon seeing Maganda the little man fairy made a most graceful bow

head, and hurried home. When she reached the edge of the village, everything had changed. New buildings stood where old ones had been when she left.

"Poor me!" she exclaimed, "those fairies have bewitched me." All the time she thought she heard:

"Time flies,
Time dies."

At last she found her home, but there everything, too, was changed. The neat little house she had left only an hour before was old and tumbling down. She pushed open the door and entered. In the room, which was lit by the dim light of one candle, an old man and an old woman were sitting.

"Please tell me," she asked after she had set the bundle of wood and the casket on the floor, "where my uncle and aunt are?"

The old people looked at her in surprise, but said kindly:

"We do not know, little one. Give us your name, and perhaps we can tell you where they live."

"Why," she replied, "my name is Maganda, and this is my home. I left here only an hour ago, and my uncle and aunt were here when I left. What can be the matter?"

"We know of no one by your name that lives in our village now," replied the old couple.

"Alas!" went on the old woman, as she began to cry, "we once had a dear little girl by that name, but twenty years ago she went into the forest to gather wood and we have never seen her since."

Suddenly the light of the candle grew brighter, and Maganda saw that the old people were her aunt and uncle. She threw her arms around their necks and told them all that had happened. When they learned that their long-lost child had returned, they wept for joy.

Maganda poured her story into their happy ears.

"And the fairy gave me this casket when I left," she ended up. "I do not know what is in it, but, perhaps, as it is so pretty, we could sell it for enough to buy us all some food, and you, dear Aunt and Uncle, some warm clothing."

She brought the casket forward and they all admired its strange beauty. Then she lifted the lid. She and the two old people stared in amazement for the casket was filled to the very top with gold and jewels worth a large fortune. When Maganda hung a necklace of pearls about her neck, there was not a princess in the whole country who was half as beautiful.

At the bottom of the casket was found a strip of parchment. Written in quaint characters were the words, "Set this casket upon the bank of the river." When Maganda carried it to the riverbank and set it down, the casket grew larger and larger until it had changed into a beautiful house. In it she lived happily with her aunt and uncle for many days.

Every few weeks, however, Maganda would run off to the forest to take part in the frolics of the banyan fairies, but she was always careful not to stay too long. Some of the people of the village say that she married the king of the fairies—and who knows!

THE SNAPPER BROTHERS

A good many years ago, there lived in a pond on the island of Luzon a couple of big snapping turtles. They were brothers, who had lived there ever since they were hatched from eggs,and laid in the warm sand at the edge of the water a hundred years before. Like all snapping turtles they were stupid and selfish. Their shells were as hard as stone, and their heads were as hard as their shells.

Before they had grown so old, the turtles got along well enough with their neighbors, the pelicans, the wild ducks, and the long-legged wading birds, but they now quarreled with them continually.

"Go away!" They said to them. "This pond is ours; we do not like to hear your honking, quacking, and clattering all the time. We cannot even take a noonday nap on account of the noise you make."

The crabbed old snappers swallowed the fluffy little duck-lings; they bit the toes of the ducks; they nipped the legs of the pelicans. Once when a large blue heron put his head into the wa-ter to pick up a snail, one of the turtles grabbed him by the bill with his strong jaws. He then pulled the heron under the water and held him until he was drowned.

"This will never do," said a wise old drake to his companions, the water birds. "I am going to ask the monkey if he cannot do something to help us get rid of our bad neighbors." So a message was sent to the monkey, who arrived in a short time.

"I think I can manage to send them away," said he to the drake when he had heard the story. "I don't like turtles myself. Only a few days ago the ugly creatures frightened my little son almost out of his wits, when he went to the pond for a drink. The poor little fellow's mother is angry about the matter, too. She's had to fetch him water in a coconut shell ever since."

One hot day about noon, when the turtles were sunning themselves upon a log that stuck out over the water, the monkey climbed to the top of a tall coconut tree which hung over the log. He pulled off the largest nut he could find, and dropped it upon the back of one of the turtles. No sooner had the nut hit him than the turtle tumbled into the water. His brother tumbled in with him.

At the bottom of the pond, the one who had been hit said: "Brother, I do believe the sun just fell out of the sky upon me. Oh, my poor back! How it hurts!"

"Let us go to the surface and see what has really happened," said the brother.

The two now crawled out upon the bank. Everything was quite dark for a cloud had just come over the face of the sun. Suddenly, the turtle who had been hit, saw the coconut sticking in the mud where it had rolled after bouncing from his back.

"Now," said he, "I told you it was the sun that fell; there it lies in the mud."

"Foolish one," said his brother, "that is not the sun; it is only a big, round rock."

"Call it a rock if you want to," said the one who had been hit "but I say it is the sun."

"Well," said the other, "let's ask the monkey. He will know what it is."

So the turtles called the monkey and asked him to tell them what the round object was. He looked at the nut closely and then

The turtles asked the monkey to tell them what the round object was

said:

"The thing is round like the sun, and yellow like the sun, but it doesn't seem to shine."

"Too bad," said the turtles, not giving the monkey time to finish. "What are we going to do for sunshine to warm ourselves? We see plainly that the sun will not shine when it is down here on the ground."

"I think I can fix the matter," said the monkey. "I shall take the sun in my arms, climb up the tree, and put it back in the sky. But you must remember that it is liable to get in the habit of falling and tumble down again in the same place."

"If that is the case," said the wounded turtle, "I am going to move to a pond where the sun will not be likely to hit me the next time it takes a notion to fall."

Upon saying these words, he set out across the country toward a lake in which lived only animals of his kind.

"Friends," said he, when he arrived, "a queer thing happened on my way a while ago; the sun dropped upon me and nearly killed me. However, I persuaded the monkey to climb a tall tree and put it back in the sky, but, sad to relate, he fears it might fall again. It seems to me that I had better move over here."

"You are welcome," said the inhabitants of the lake, "but we think you are a little queer in the head. Where is your brother?"

"He wouldn't come," said the visitor. "He doubted that it was the sun that had fallen, after he'd had time to think the matter over. I hated to leave him over there in such a dangerous place, but he always did think he knew more than anyone else."

Now the brother who stayed behind thought all the time that it was the sun that had fallen, but he was stubborn, and wouldn't leave because he knew quite well that the water birds wanted him to go. He wouldn't sleep upon the log any more in the daytime, however, though he had no fear about sleeping upon it at night.

Now, when the moon was full in the sky and shining directly above the sleeping turtle, the monkey waited until a small cloud hid its face. Then he climbed up the tree again and, taking careful aim, he dropped a big coconut upon him. The turtle tumbled into the water, moaning with pain. In a little while he called out to the monkey:

"I know it was not the sun that fell this time, because it is night. It must have been the moon. Oh, my poor back! Oh, my back!"

"If it were the moon that fell," said the monkey, "it must be floating in the water under the log. Bring it to me so that I can put it back in the sky."

The foolish old turtle brought the coconut and gave it to the monkey.

"Put the moon back in its place, if you like," he said, "but I'm going to my brother. Goodbye!"

He now set out at once to look for his brother. He had not gone far when he met him, on his way back.

"Let's return to our old home," said the one who thought he had been hit by the sun. "My new neighbors all say I am crazy for thinking the sun fell. Perhaps I was mistaken."

"Well," said the one who thought he had been hit by the moon, "it might not have been the sun that struck you, but I know it was the moon that fell upon me. You may return if you want to, but as for me I am going on to the place you have just left."

"I shall go with you," said the other hastily; and off they set, side by side, for the lake in which lived only animals of their kind. Next day when the new visitor showed a dent in his shell, and told about the moon falling, every turtle in the lake believed his story, as well as the story of the first visitor.

Never afterward would either of the Snapper Brothers venture near their old home, nor would any other turtle go near it, to the great joy of the pelicans, the ducks, and the herons, who now had the pond all to themselves. And to this day their grandchildren and great-grandchildren are living there in peace and happiness.

THE PARADISE OF THE ANIMALS

Club tail, the buffalo, lay in his wallow one evening at the close of a hard day's work at the plow.

"My old master," he thought, "always treated me kindly. Every morning he sent his boy to pull tender grass so that I might eat my fill at the noon hour. He never prodded me with a sharp goad, and was careful not to jerk the rope fastened to the ring in my nose. When he unhitched me he patted my shoulders and said, 'Good old ox, if it had not been for you my family would have starved long ago. But alas! Things have changed since my good master died. His son prods me until my back is sore... and as for my poor nose, he jerks the rope so that I am afraid the ring will be torn from it. Instead of tender grass at noon, all I get now is a bundle of stale rice straw, and at night when I am unhitched my young master kicks me and says, 'Stupid one, if you were not so old and tough I would sell you to the butcher.'"

Club Tail scrambled from the mire to graze in the rice stubble. When the bright moon came up over the tall palm trees, he said to himself, "I am going away to the mountains where no people live, and I will find a valley with bright pools of water and tender grass. There I can live in peace the rest of my days." So, about midnight, he started, wading up a shallow stream towards the mountains.

"This river," he said, "will cover up all signs of my tracks, and as tomorrow is a feast day, I shall be hidden away in the mountains before my cruel young master knows that I am gone."

By noon the next day Club Tail was far up in the foothills, but he no longer waded in the river. As he trudged along a path on the bank, a zebu came out from a near-by field.

"Hello, yoke brother," greeted the zebu, "where are you going?" "I am on my way to the mountains where no people live," replied the buffalo. It is all on account of the cruel treatment of my young master."

"I wish I could go with you," said Humpy Lump, the zebu. "Only yesterday my young master made me trot all day under the whip, while I was hitched to a heavy cart. Oh! My back still smarts from the whiplashes, and my bones ache from so much trotting,"

"Come with me," answered Club Tail, "I shall be glad to have your company." The two animals had not gone far when they met an old ram, freshly sheared, with his sides bleeding from cuts.

"Whither away, Brother Grass Eaters?" asked the ram.

"We are on our way to the mountains where no people live," replied Club Tail and Humpy Lump. "It is all on account of cruel treatment from our young masters."

"Let me go with you," begged Wrinkle Sides, the ram. "This morning when my young master sheared me, he cut off great pieces of my skin, and said I deserved to have more of it taken off because I was so old and wrinkled. How can I help being old and wrinkled?"

"Come with us," said the two oxen, "we shall be glad to have your company."

Further on they met an old goat with blue whiskers. He seemed very angry about something. He asked, "Where are you going, Brother Grass Eaters?"

"We are on our way to the mountains where no people live," replied the three companions. "It is all on account of cruel treatment from our young masters."

"If you are not ashamed of me I wish you would let me come with you," said Blue Whiskers, the goat. "It was only an hour ago that my young master spoiled my beautiful white beard by dipping it into a vat of indigo. What could be uglier than a goat with blue whiskers!"

Tree Horns came to guide the animals to the place the monkey had told them about

"Come with us," said the other animals, "we shall be glad to have your company."

That night the four travelers stopped in a coconut grove at the foot of a high mountain, where they decided to sleep. Before they lay down, the wise monkey, called Mr. Monk by the jungle people, came down from a tall tree to greet them.

"Where are you bound, tame folks?" he asked, "and what seems to be the trouble? I judge from your looks that things have not gone well with you."

Each traveler told his story, and Mr. Monk said he was sorry to hear of the bad treatment they had received from their young masters. But when he looked at the long, blue whiskers of the goat, he could hardly keep from smiling.

"You were right," he said after a pause, "to flee from your cruel masters. Rest here until morning, and I will have Tree Horns, the deer, lead you to a place of safety."

"Thank you, Mr. Monk," said the animals. They then lay down and were soon busy chewing their cuds.

Next morning Tree Horns came to guide the animals to the place the monkey had told them about. Before sundown they had reached a valley surrounded by high cliffs. In the middle of the valley there was a pleasant lake with shade trees on its banks, while tender grass grew all around it.

"We could not have found a prettier place," said the tired old grass eaters, "but are you sure that man never comes here?" they questioned anxiously.

"I am sure of that," replied Tree Horns. "There is but one entrance to this valley, and man will never be able to find it, because it is hidden by thick vines." Saying this the deer bade the animals goodbye and went back to his home in the jungles of the lowlands.

The four companions found everything to their liking. No man ever came to trouble them. Every day when they had eaten their fill of the tender grass and drunk deep of the cool, clear water of the lake, they lay down in the shade of the grove to rest. Club Tail spent a great deal of his time bathing, for he liked to soak his thick, spongy hide in the cool water.

After living there a year the animals sent for others of their kind and there, with their children and grandchildren, they are living in contentment to this very day, and no man has ever come upon them.

LITTLE CROOKEDBILL

An old wild duck once sat upon nine eggs, which she had laid in a nest among the reeds at the edge of a pretty lake. In the lake grew many lily pads whose flowers were almost as large as the nest that she sat upon. The palms dipped their broad leaves into the waters, the birds sang all day in the nearby trees, and the frogs kept the music going at night.

"What a fine place to raise a family!" thought the old duck. "There are no turtles in the beautiful lake, neither do cats nor other bird-eating animals ever come near."

While she was thus musing, she heard a faint peep beneath her wings, and she quacked aloud with joy. In a little while a duckling came out of the eggshell. Then, one by one, the eight other eggs burst open, and from each came a duckling.

"That was a wonderful hatch!" thought the mother duck, "but it all came about through good care and quiet surroundings. I know all my children will be obedient."

Next day the old duck stood upon the bank looking at her children.

"What pretty soft down they have," she said, "and such lovely yellow bills, and pretty pink toes, and how they turn up their eyes! And such swimmers I never saw in all my life!"

The nine little ducks swam all day long, and at night huddled under their mother's wings.

When the ducklings were almost ready to fly their mother said to them: "Children, you must never go to the muddy lake across the marsh. In it lives a great old snapping turtle, and he would be sure to catch you."

"Oh, no, Mother," said the little ducks, "we shall never put our feet in the muddy lake."

When the ducklings were a month or two older, their mother let them fly away for short periods by themselves. They now thought they knew almost as much as their mother. One time she scolded them for staying away so long.

"I hope," she said, "that you have not been near the lake where the turtle lives."

"We never went into the lake, Mother," they said.

That was true, but all nine of them had stood upon the bank and looked for the turtle.

"Mother is mistaken," they thought, "because we saw nothing but frogs and fishes in the lake. Really, the lake is not so muddy, either. We think it is prettier than ours. How we wish we could go swimming in it."

Next morning the duckling who had done most of the talking flew away to the lake by himself. He stood upon the banks and looked for the turtle, but could not see him. First he stood upon one foot, then upon the other, and then upon both feet. At length he said to himself: "I'll just take a little swim in the lake. Mother will never know what I did."

He jumped into the lake, and swam and swam until his legs were tired. He then started toward the bank intending to hop out and fly home to his mother. Just as he was about to do so he saw a frog, and put his head under the water to catch him. As he did so the turtle caught him by the beak in his strong jaws, and pulled him to the bottom of the lake. There he bit him on the head until he thought he had killed the duckling. The turtle then started to eat him, first taking him by the toes and crushing them. As the turtle did this, the duck gave a mighty struggle and freed himself. He rose to the top, swam to the bank, and climbed out, almost dead. After he had lain there a long time, he arose with much difficulty and flew home.

When his mother saw him, she burst into tears, for the duckling's bill and toes were so terribly crooked. She walked away among the reeds and put her head under her wing.

The duckling soon got well, but his bill and toes never grew straight again, and every time he tried to quack, he made a harsh, squawking sound. Ever after his companions called him Crooked-bill.

Crookedbill would never go into the water again, and as all the other ducks laughed at him when he tried to quack, he became so unhappy that he flew away into the forest and never returned. There he married a tree bird who soon afterward laid two eggs. From the eggs hatched two birds with squawking voices, crooked bills, and crooked toes like their father's. And that is how the parrot family began.

MR. MONK AND MR. TERRAPIN

The Philippine land terrapin is much larger than the American variety The Philippine monkey does not hold on to limbs with his tail. Asiatic monkeys cannot use their tails for grasping. That is a property which belongs to the new-world variety.

A terrapin once stole some bananas. He was carrying them along the hot, dusty road when a monkey sitting high among the branches of a tree called out to him:

"Will you give me a few of your bananas?"

"Beggar, why do you not work for your own bananas as I do?" replied the terrapin.

"I will, if you will give me a job," answered the monkey.

"I have no work for you to do," snapped the terrapin. "Besides if I did, I would not hire you, because you are so lazy."

"No, I am not," said the monkey. "Now, really, could you not spare at least a couple of your bananas to a poor, hungry brother? You have so many that half of them will spoil before you can eat them."

"In that case I shall throw them away," replied the stingy terrapin.

"Friend," said the monkey, changing the subject, "do you know that it is mighty nice and cool up here, and you cannot imagine how beautiful the view is. Why, over there to the north I can see a, ship in full sail, and its flag tells me it is from a strange land. As I look to the south I see a great city with a wall around it; the king of man has his palace there. In a wide valley on the east the farmers are gathering the rice, and far, far to the west there is a grand old mountain with silvery clouds about its peak; and oh, such a lovely waterfall is leaping down its sides!"

The foolish terrapin was so pleased by this speech that he stood upon his hind legs and poked out his head until it looked like the knot in the end of a rope. Gazing up to the monkey, he said: "I wish I could climb. Do you think you could teach me? "

"Of course I could," said the monkey.

"All right, you may begin," said the terrapin. He left the bananas and started toward the tree.

"Very well," replied the monkey, "but you must remember that I always charge my pupils for their lessons. Give me six bananas and I shall teach you to climb up here where I am."

"That is too many," said the terrapin.

"Give me four, then," said the monkey, trying to close the bargain.

"No," said the terrapin.

"Two, then," said the monkey.

"No, but I shall give you one if you'll let me pick it out," said the terrapin.

"All right," said the monkey, and he came down the tree.

The terrapin picked out a little banana about the size of a baby's finger and handed it to the monkey. The monkey ate it, but it was so green that he wished he had left it alone.

" Are you ready?" asked the monkey after he had eaten the banana.

"I am," said the terrapin.

"Take hold of the end of my tail with your mouth, then," ordered the monkey, "and when we start stick your claws into the bark of the tree and don't forget to move your legs as if you were walking."

The monkey began to climb the tree with the terrapin hanging to his tail. When he had gone about halfway, he said to the terrapin:

"Knot-head, why don't you help a little? You are so heavy that my tail is being pulled out by the roots."

The terrapin only grinned as he drew his clublike feet farther into his shell.

Up, up, they went until they were at the very top of the tree.

The monkey placed his pupil in a crow's nest, slid to the ground, and sat down beside the bananas.

In a little while the terrapin said " I have seen quite enough for this time, you may now teach me how to climb down," but when he looked around the monkey was nowhere to be seen. When the terrapin spied him on the ground beside the bananas, he became very angry. " Come back up here, old Crinkle Tail, and teach me how to get down," he demanded in harsh tones.

"Say, now, Mr. Terrapin, you are very ill-mannered toward your teacher," replied Mr. Monk.

"Did I not pay you to teach me to climb?" growled the terrapin.

"Oh, ho!" laughed the monkey. "I agreed to teach you how to climb up the tree, but there was nothing said about teaching you to climb down. That comes in the second lesson."

The terrapin was so angry that his shell almost cracked, but the monkey only laughed at him.

"How many bananas will you take to teach me this second lesson?" the terrapin finally asked, as he saw that he could gain nothing through anger.

"A dozen," answered the monkey.

"That's too many," said the terrapin.

"How about half a dozen," said the monkey.

"Too many still," said the terrapin.

"Give me three, then," said the monkey.

"I will not," snapped the terrapin, "but I will give you two if you will let me pick them out."

"All right," said the monkey. Then after a pause, he shouted, "Jump Down!"

Mr. Monk then took the whole bunch of bananas, which the terrapin had stolen and walked away laughing.

So far as anyone knows, that stingy old terrapin is still up in the tree.

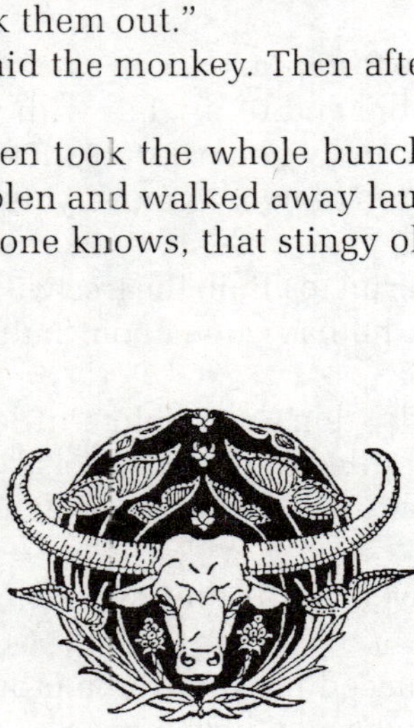

THE MEDDLESOME PIGGY

A monkey, a dog, and a cat once made an agreement that they would always be friends.

"Let's find ourselves a house," said the monkey.

"Good," said the dog.

"Good," said the cat.

So they found a house in the forest, and went to live in it.

"I'll get the food," said the dog.

"I'll be the cook," said the monkey.

"I'll sweep the house," said the cat.

So the dog got the food, the monkey cooked the meals, and the cat swept the house.

After the three animals had lived together in peace for a whole year, they decided to give a big dinner to celebrate their happiness.

The dog went out to get food; the monkey went out to get some dry sticks to make a fire; the cat stayed at home to sweep the house.

While the dog and the monkey were gone, a pig came along and saw the house. The door was open. He walked in.

"Get out of my clean house, you dirty pig!" said the cat.

But the pig would not leave. He turned the table over. He put his nose into the cooking pots. He ate up all the food there was in the house. He then lay down in the monkey's bed and went to sleep.

"I must run and tell the monkey and the dog about the dirty pig," said the cat. "We must run him away. I do not want a dirty pig in our pretty clean house."

The cat soon found the monkey and the dog. The monkey was carrying some sticks of wood in his arms. The dog was carrying some food in his mouth.

"Oh," said the cat, "there's a pig in our house. He turned the table over. He put his nose into the cooking pots. He ate up all the food. He then went to sleep in the monkey's bed."

The monkey, the dog, and the cat ran home as fast as they could. They sat down on the grass near the door to think how to drive the pig away.

After a while the cat said, "I'll twist his tail." "I'll bite his ears," said the dog.

"I'll hit him on the nose with a stick," said the monkey.

They all went into the house. The pig was still asleep in the monkey's bed. They slipped up to the bed.

The cat twisted the pig's tail. The dog bit his ears. The monkey gave him a hard lick on the nose.

"Wee! Wee!" squealed the pig, as he ran out of the door. He ran into the woods, and never came back again. But his tail is still curly, because the cat twisted it. His ears still hang down, because the dog bit them. And the end of his nose is still flat, because the monkey hit it with a stick.

MR. MONK AND THE SMART YOUNG TORTOISES

A couple of young tortoises once found a clump of banana sprouts that a farmer had lost in the road. As the tortoises had seen a man setting out from a banana grove, they thought they knew all about such matters, so they decided to start a grove for themselves.

As each of the tortoises came upon the clump at the same time, and thought it contained but a single sprout, each claimed it, and so began to quarrel. At length both seized the bunch of sprouts and started down the road with it between them, fighting and quarreling as they went.

It was not long before the tortoises passed beneath the tree in which Mr. Monk lived. The monkey, upon hearing the commotion, came down to see what was the matter.

"What is the trouble?" he asked.

"This banana sprout is mine, because I found it first," declared each of the tortoises at the same time. They then let go of the clump and began to fight.

"Well," said Mr. Monk, "I see no reason for all this fuss. The clump contains four sprouts; why not divide them between you?

In this way you can each start a banana grove."

"We hadn't thought of that," answered the tortoises, "but how can we divide them?"

"I shall show you," returned the monkey, "if you will stop your quarreling."

"We promise you that we shall not quarrel any more, if you can divide the clump so that each of us will have two sprouts," said the tortoises.

Mr. Monk sat down and carefully pulled the sprouts apart, and then gave two to each tortoise.

Each threw his trees over his shoulders and started away, without so much as thanking the monkey for settling their quarrel. When they had gone a little way down the road, both turned round and shouted:

"When our trees begin to bear, come over, old Crinkle Tail, and we shall give you some bananas to eat. You may have the bad ones that we won't want." They then went on their way laughing, and the monkey climbed back to the limb where he usually slept.

"We'll see who'll eat the bad bananas," said he to himself as he stretched out for a nap.

The tortoises carefully dug holes in the ground and set out the trees. In due time the trees began to bear fruit, and the tortoises looked up each day to see if the fruit was ripe; but they never once thought how they were to reach the ripe fruit.

When one of the bunches was yellow, the monkey came along and found both tortoises standing under the tree looking up at the fruit. Without asking permission he climbed the tree, sat down comfortably among the leaves, and pulled off a big, yellow banana. After he had eaten all he wanted, he found an over-ripe banana on the bunch, pulled it off and threw it down to the tortoises.

"My friends," he said, "you see who it is that gets the bad fruit. Had you been grateful for what I did to help you a year or more ago, I would have been content to accept a few of these good bananas for my trouble. As it is you will have to put up with whatever I throw down to you, or go without any fruit at all."

LEETIE AND THE WOOD FAIRIES

Once upon a time a tiny baby girl was born to a poor washerman and his wife. The child was no larger than her mother's thumb. When the neighbors came to see her they all exclaimed, "Maleeit-eeit!" which in English means, "My, how little!"

The mother upon hearing this exclamation decided to name her baby *Maleeit-eeit;* but as the word was so long she shortened it to Leetie, and ever after the child was called Leetie.

When Leetie was six years old she was no larger than a doll. All the children of the neighborhood, as well as the grown people, wished to play with her; but her mother was afraid she would be hurt, so she seldom allowed her to play with anyone.

Now Leetie was an active child, and she wanted to play as other children did. One night as she was going to bed, she said:

"Mother, I wish a little fairy would come here and live with us. Then I would be happy, because I would have someone to play with that would not hurt me."

"Let us hope that your wish may come true," replied the mother as she tucked Leetie in her tiny bed.

The next morning Leetie went with her parents to the river, where they washed the clothes. She played about in the clean, white sand and pebbles until she grew tired, then she wandered off a short distance upon the green banks to gather wild flowers. Soon a great butterfly settled upon a flower to sip the nectar. Leetie thought the butterfly was the prettiest creature she had ever seen. She longed to play with him. The butterfly, however, was timid, and whenever Leetie came near him he would flit away to another flower. She followed him to the edge of the woods. Here he disappeared. Leetie now turned around and ran as fast as her little legs could carry her in the direction of her parents as she thought. But she was really going in the opposite direction. On she ran until she was quite out of breath. At length she sat down upon a tuft of soft, green moss to rest. As she was sitting there crying, a great grasshopper came along, saw her, and asked:

"What is the matter, little fairy?"

"I am lost," she cried, "please take me to my father and mother."

"That I shall," replied the grasshopper kindly, for he thought she was a little wood fairy who had lost her way. He picked her up in his arms, and started off at a swinging trot, saying:

"You are a long way from home. How is it that you got so far away?"

"I was trying to catch the pretty butterfly," replied Leetie, with tears in her eyes, "but he was afraid I would hurt him, so he flew off and I followed him. Please hurry, Mr. Grasshopper, because my father and mother will be worried."

"I shall go as fast as I can," replied the grasshopper, "but even then it will take me until the middle of the afternoon to reach your home, for you have traveled many miles away from it."

Then he began to run and hop as fast as he could, but he was careful not to hurt the wee little girl in his arms. After a while Leetie went to sleep and did not awaken until they had come to the place in the midst of the deep forest where the wood fairies lived. The grasshopper set her down near a great mushroom, larger than the largest umbrella, and said, "Here's where the fairies live. You can ask some of the little fairy children where your home is." The grasshopper then took several long hops and disappeared into the woods.

A number of little tree fairy boys and girls were sliding down the side of the great mushroom into the soft sand below. When they saw Leetie they were greatly surprised. Leetie was surprised, too; so much so that for a time she forgot she was lost. Two little fairies took her by the hands and helped her to climb to the top of the mushroom. Soon she was enjoying the sport of coasting more than any of the rest, for this was the first time in her whole life that she had ever had a chance to play with children like herself.

After a while the tree fairy mothers came from their homes in the trees nearby to call their children to supper, and when they saw Leetie they were surprised and wondered where she had come from. They were sure they knew every little tree fairy in the whole forest. A messenger was sent to the king to tell him of the strange child among them. When the king appeared, he found Leetie and his own little son playing as happily as if they had known each other all their lives. He asked the little prince about Leetie, but all the prince knew was that a grasshopper had brought her!

Leetie now thought of her parents, and began to cry to be taken home.

"Who are your parents, pretty one?" asked the king, "and where do they live?"

"My parents are poor people, and they live in the town," sobbed Leetie.

"That cannot be," said the king greatly puzzled, "for the world people do not have little fairy girls like you. Tell me the name of this town."

Leetie did not know the name of the town where she lived, but said it had a great church, with a red roof and a high tower with a cross on top.

"This is, indeed, very strange," said the king. "It is hard to believe that you are the daughter of world people, but it must be, for you do not belong to any of us. I know every fairy, young and old, that lives in the forest. It is plain, too, that you have seen the home of the world people."

The fairy king's house was in a giant bamboo tree, the tallest of all the trees. He took Leetie in his arms and climbed to the very top of the tree, which was so tall that it reached almost to the clouds. He asked the little girl to look out through the leaves and tell him if she could see the town where she lived. The sun was just setting, and flooded by its glory Leetie saw in the distance the great red roof of the church, and the tower with its bright cross.

"Oh, there is where I live! " she exclaimed.

The king now called a servant and told him to bring a couple of swift flying foxes. When the foxes had been brought, he bade the nurse of the little prince to mount one of them and placed Leetie on the other. Then he commanded the foxes to go to the town as fast as they could.

Now when they were ready, Leetie cried for the little prince to go with her. She begged so hard that the king finally said he might go. So the prince and Leetie mounted one of the flying foxes and the nurse the other, and away they flew over the tree tops. At first Leetie was afraid she would fall off, but the fairy prince, who was used to such rides, held her fast, and told her there was no danger.

When they arrived at the town where Leetie lived not a, person, young or old, could be found, for they had all left their homes to look for the wee bit of a girl.

Leetie begged the nurse to let the little prince stay with her at home until morning. The nurse did not like to do this, but at, last she consented, saying she would come back in the morning for the prince.

The next day, just as the sun was coming up, the washerman and his wife, sad of heart and weeping, came home, thinking that their little daughter was lost forever. When they saw Leetie asleep, words could not express their joy. In another room was the little fairy prince, and upon seeing him the mother forgot all her sadness and began to laugh, because she thought Leetie would now have a playmate,and that her wish had come true.

Later in the day, the nurse returned for the prince, bringing some gifts for the poor parents. The little girl had such a joyous day playing with the little prince that she cried as if her heart would break when the time came for him to go home. And the prince cried to stay with Leetie. The nurse, however, had to take him home, where he was very unhappy and lonesome without Leetie.

The fairy king, seeing how fond of the little girl his son was, and how unhappy he was without her, visited Leetie's parents, who agreed that Leetie might live half the year with the fairies if the little prince would live the other half at Leetie's home. Leetie was now the happiest child in the world, because she had a playmate, and the little prince was just as happy.

When they were grown up, there was a grand wedding in the old church with the red roof, for the prince and Leetie were married there. Then they went to the forest to live with the fairies, but Leetie never forgot her parents. She would often visit them in the fine house she had built for them.

When the old king died, the prince and Leetie became king and queen of the fairies, and for all I know, are living in the forest to this day, in great peace and happiness.

THE TIMID LITTLE HERMIT CRAB

'Fraid boy, come out!
Why do you pout?
No use to cry,
Show your eye.

Oh, there he goes
On tiny toes
Making a track;
House on his back.

What does he write
In sand so white?
"I'm shy, I'm shy;
Goodbye, goodbye!"

THE CLEVER LITTLE HERMIT CRAB

Once upon a time a big old crab, that lived where the river flowed into the sea, was walking upon the sandy beach, when he met a coconut crab. The two at once got into an argument as to which was the more clever.

"My only real enemy," said the river crab, "is man. When I see a man, I make for the water with all speed, and tumble in, or else I scuttle into a hole, and that is the end of it. Often, it is true, the more simple creatures of my tribe are caught in crab pots, but I know all such devices, and so I never worry about them," continued the rusty old fellow, holding up one of his strong claws. "I can even cope with man. Did I not once nip off a man's finger with these very pincers of mine! As to taking food," boasted the river crab, "no other creature is better fitted than I. Not only have I strong pincers with teeth in them, but my jaws are well equipped for crushing things."

"What you say," replied the coconut crab, "may be true, but in case there is no deep water, or a hole near, you are likely to be caught when a man appears. I can do all you can, and besides, I can climb a tree. As to strong claws, you do not have the better of me. I have been known to break a man's arm with mine, while all you were able to do was to pinch off a finger. As to taking food, I can strip off the toughest covering of a coconut, punch out its eyes' and scoop out the meat. So you see, brother, I am far more clever than you."

This talk made the river crab so angry that he attacked the coconut crab furiously. As the two were fighting, a comic little fiddler crab came up and began to play his fiddle. His music attracted the two larger creatures, and they at once stopped fighting to listen. When the fiddler had played several tunes, he said:

"Well, boys, I heard all your arguments, but there is no use to fight over the matter; neither of you is half as clever as I am."

The two big crabs were so amused at the little fiddler that they forgot their disagreement and began to laugh.

"Mr. Fiddler," they said, "what other thing can you do besides being able to stop a fight with your music? "

"I," replied the fiddler, "always have a number of holes dug on the salty banks, into which I can scuttle sideways in case of danger. My larger claw not only serves me for taking food, fighting, and such things, but it also makes an excellent fiddle with which to while away the dreary hours. You big fellows do not know how to amuse yourselves except by fighting."

At this interesting point of the argument, a little hermit crab came rattling along over the sands.

"Ho!" he exclaimed, "I heard what you fellows had to say, but all of you put together are not as clever as I. I carry my house upon my back, and all I have to do when threatened by danger is to withdraw into my shell house. While my claws are not even as strong as the fiddler's, they serve me quite well for taking whatever food I need."

Upon hearing this, the two big crabs became angry and darted toward the hermit crab, with wide-open pincers. The hermit crab at once withdrew into his hard shell, and laughed while the big fellows tried to crush him. At length the river crab broke off one of the prongs of his right claw, and while he moaned with pain a fisherman came up, threw his net over him and carried him home, where he was served up the next day for the fisherman's dinner.

The coconut crab escaped by climbing the nearest tree, while the fiddler scuttled into the nearest hole. All the hermit did was to lie still a few moments, then put out his legs and crawl away.

Next day the three remaining crabs met and resumed the argument. Scarcely had they begun when the fisherman returned with a lasso. Getting between the crabs and the tree, the fisherman threw the lasso over the coconut crab, caught him, and took him home. There the crab was fed upon coconut meat until he was fat; then he, too, was served up for the fisherman's dinner.

The fiddler and the hermit later on met again. "It is very clear," said the fiddler, "that we are both more clever than the river crab and the coconut crab, for their enemy has already caught them. I still contend, however, that a hole in the ground is a safer place than a shell on one's back. Something might swallow you shell and all. Then what could you do?"

Just as the fiddler finished speaking, a long-billed heron swooped down upon him. The fiddler at once ran into a hole, while the hermit withdrew into his shell. The heron poked his long bill into the hole, and drew out the unfortunate fiddler and after pulling off his one large pincer, swallowed him.

Looking around, the heron espied the hermit crab who had poked out his eyes in time to see his companion swallowed.

"Well," said the bird, "I need a bit of shell to help digest what I have just eaten, so I'll swallow the hermit here."

So saying, he gobbled up the hermit crab. When the two were inside the heron's crop, the fiddler said sadly:

"Alas, friend, neither of us was clever when it came to escaping from the heron."

"Never mind," answered the little hermit, "just wait until this fellow alights, and I will show you where my real cleverness comes in."

Soon after the heron alighted in a rice field. The hermit then stuck out his pincers and ripped open the bird's crop, as though it had been a piece of paper. The two crabs at once fell out, while the bird flew away screaming. The hermit now took the wounded fiddler upon his back and carried him to his home, where he waited a long time for a new claw to grow.

"Well," said the fiddler one day, after he had recovered, "I will have to admit that you are the cleverest of all the crab family."

GOOTOM AND THE TREE FAIRY

Once upon a time there lived a poor woodcutter. Every day he hitched his ox to his cart and went into the forest for a load of wood, which he sold in the village. Thus he was able to buy food and clothes for his large family.

After a time the poor man became ill and died, leaving no money. His widow had to work very hard to get food for herself and her children. One day the woman said to her oldest son. "Gootom, you are now twelve years old. Take the ox and go into the forest as your father used to do and bring home a load of wood."

Gootom did as his mother told him. He chopped a load by the middle of the afternoon, for he was big and strong for his age. When his cart was full, he noticed a fine tree nearby, and decided to chop it down, too, before going home. By doing this he would be able to take two loads of wood to town the next day.

He had chopped but a few minutes when he heard a voice. It seemed to come from the branches of the tree. Looking up, he saw a little old fairy half-hidden by the leaves.

"Gootom," she said, "do not chop down my pretty home, do not chop down my pretty home. There are plenty of other trees that will do for wood. Please go away and let me alone."

Gootom was surprised to learn that the tree was the home of a fairy, but he said:

"This is a nice straight tree with many limbs, and I am sure it will be easy to chop and split. You can move to an old crooked tree, which will do you just as well for a home."

"No," replied the fairy, "I do not want to do that. I have lived here a hundred years, and old fairies, like old people, do not like to move from their homes. Hark you," the fairy continued, "I will give you a magic deer trap. Set it in the forest every evening. The next morning you will find a deer in it; if the trap does not work, you may come back and cut down my tree."

Gootom was greatly pleased. He took the trap, climbed upon his cart and started home. On the way he stopped at the house of a farmer, named Bobo. When he saw the trap he said:

"That is a fine trap, Gootom. Where did you get it?"

"A tree fairy gave it to me," replied the boy. "All you have to do is to set it in the evening and the next morning there will be a deer in it."

When Bobo heard what the trap would do, he wanted it for himself and planned a way to get it. He asked Gootom to come in and rest himself. Then, while Mrs. Bobo told Gootom a long story Bobo stole the trap and took it out to his tool shed, where he made another that looked exactly like the real one. When he had finished it, he went back into the house, and placed the false trap where Gootom had left his magic one. Gootom took the false trap and went home.

When he told his mother about his magic trap, she smiled and said, " I am afraid the fairy played a joke on you, but after you sell the wood you may set the trap if you wish."

Gootom hurried away, sold the wood and gave the money to his mother. He then took his trap out to the edge of the forest and set it. Early next morning, before the sun was up, he hastened to see if he had caught a deer; but when he reached the place he found that the trap had nothing in it.

Hurrying home he hitched up his ox, and went back to the spot where he had chopped the load of wood the day before. He began to chop at the fairy's tree.

The fairy appeared a second time, and said: "What are you doing, Gootom? Did I not give you the magic deer trap so that you would let me alone? Go away, and let me live in peace!"

"The trap you gave me was no good," replied Gootom. "I set it as you told me, but this morning when I went to get the deer there was no deer in it."

"That is indeed strange," said the fairy. " Give me another chance. This time I shall give you a magic pocket. Sew it into your clothing, and every morning when you awake there will be a piece of gold in it. If you do not find the gold, come tomorrow morning and chop down my tree."

Gootom took the pocket, chopped his load of wood from another tree nearby and departed.

On his way home he stopped again at the house of Bobo.

"How did your trap work?" asked Bobo.

"It was no good," replied Gootom, "but the fairy gave me a magic pocket that will have a piece of gold in it every morning," and he drew forth his gift.

When Bobo heard this he began to plan how he might get it also. He begged Gootom to lay aside the pocket and have something to eat and drink before continuing on his way. While he and Gootom were eating, Mrs. Bobo stole the pocket and made another that looked like the real one. Gootom took the pocket that Bobo's wife had made and went home.

"Look, Mother," he said as he held up the pocket, "every morning when I put my hand in this I shall find a piece of gold."

"Son," replied the mother, "I'm afraid you are a silly boy to let the fairy fool you twice. Run along and sell the wood; it is getting late and there is no food in the house."

Before going to bed Gootom sewed the pocket into his clothing, but next morning when he put his hand in it he found it empty.

Gootom was very angry and set off as soon as possible for the forest. When he reached the tree where the fairy lived he began to chop at it vigorously. At the first stroke the fairy appeared and said, "O, Gootom, why do you chop my tree when I gave you the magic pocket to leave me alone."

"The pocket you gave me was no good," replied Gootom as he tore it from his clothing and threw it on the ground.

"I see, I see," said the fairy, when she examined the pocket, "You have some enemies that have stolen the things I gave you."

She then questioned Gootom closely, and he told her about stopping at Bobo's.

Gootom took the Magic Pocket from the Fairy

"Give me one more chance," said the fairy. "This time I shall give you a magic stick. Take it to the house of Bobo and say, "Stick, stick, beat my enemies until they are black and blue. Do as I tell you and you will soon have your trap and pocket again."

Gootom took the queer-looking stick and, not waiting to chop any wood, hastened back to Bobo's house.

Now Bobo had nearly ready a great feast of roast deer meat, to which he had invited all his relatives and friends. When he saw Gootom he became alarmed, fearing the boy would guess how he had come to have so much deer meat when deer were scarce in the forest. Though he did not want to, he invited the boy in. Some of the company, upon seeing the stick, asked questions about it.

"It is the funniest stick you ever heard of," said Gootom, while Bobo's guests began to gather around to look at it. "All you have to do, if you have an enemy, is to tell the stick to beat him."

Stepping into the middle of the floor, he said, "I am sure you would all like to see how my stick works!"

Gootom then held the stick far above his head and called out, " Stick, stick, beat my enemies until they are black and blue!"

No sooner had he said this, than the stick jumped out of his hand and struck Bobo a hard blow. It then hopped over to his wife and hit her between the shoulders. Back and forth the stick flew between Bobo and his wife, striking first one and then the other. The two thieves howled terribly, while Gootom stood by laughing.

"Please, Gootom," cried the thieves, "tell the stick to stop, and we shall give you the trap and the pocket that we stole from you. Be quick! Be quick!"

Gootom then bade the stick to stop beating the wicked pair, and they ran away groaning to get the trap and the pocket.

The boy took his property and went on his way rejoicing. He built a fine home for his mother, brothers, and sisters, near enough to the tree fairy to protect her from the woodcutters. So it came about that they all lived in peace and plenty ever after.

MR. MONK AND GRANDPA SNOUT

An old hog used to steal into a village at night to eat the banana peelings and other refuse that the people had thrown away. Early one morning as he was going back to his home in the woods, he met a monkey.

"Mr. Monk,' he said, "I've heard that you are a wise fellow; would you mind telling me how to make banana peelings?"

"Make banana peelings!" laughed the monkey. "People do not make banana peelings; they grow on trees."

"Show me a banana-peeling tree," grunted the silly old hog. The monkey was so amused at the thought of a banana-peeling tree that he lay down in the grass and laughed. Then a clever idea came to him.

"Come along," he said when he got up. "I'll take you to a whole grove of them. I am on my way there now to get my breakfast."

"Then you like banana peelings, too," said the hog.

The monkey did not answer.

He led the hog to a banana grove at the edge of a valley. He climbed up a tree that had a bunch of yellow fruit at the top.

Pulling a large banana from the bunch, he quickly stripped off the skin and threw it down to the hog, while he ate the soft pulp himself.

As the monkey was cramming his mouth with bananas, he looked through the leaves toward the village, and saw a farmer's boy riding a pony in the direction of the grove. The boy carried a long blowgun over his shoulder.

The monkey knew it was time for him to escape, for that very farmer's boy with that very blowgun had shot a hard ball of mud at him only the morning before. Without saying a word to the hog, who was under the tree gobbling up the banana peelings, the monkey leaped from tree to tree until he came to the edge of the forest. Here he climbed to the top of a tall rubber tree and hid himself among the thick leaves.

When the boy saw the hog, he put a ball of clay the size of a marble in his gun. Placing the breech to his lips he puffed out his cheeks and gave a hard blow. Zip! Went the ball, striking the hog in his side.

"Wush! Wush!" said the hog, and he started to run. As he passed beneath the rubber tree the monkey called out:

"Wait a minute, I want to tell you something."

But the hog was so terribly frightened that he did not stop.

A few days later the monkey met the hog again. "I do not think I shall ever go back to the banana-peeling grove," said the hog. "It is true that the peelings there are fresher than those in the village, but I prefer to eat bad ones in peace than fresh ones where at any moment I am in danger of being shot with a blowgun."

"Listen to me," said the monkey. "If you'll do what I tell you, we shall both have more banana peelings than we know what to do with, and not have to fear blowguns, either. I have just come from the grove. The farmer has been setting out a lot of new trees, and as he had more trees than he needed he left the extra ones on the ground. Tonight, you go and get all the trees you can carry and bring them over to the foot of the mountain. I shall teach you how to set them out and care for them. When the trees are grown I shall climb them every day and toss down to you all the peelings you can eat."

"Ugh, ugh," grunted the hog as he started toward the grove.

"What's your hurry?" said the monkey.

"Did you not tell me to fetch the banana-peeling trees?"

"I did," said the monkey, " but unless you wish to be hit by another ball from the blowgun, you had better wait till the sun goes down."

"Ugh, ugh," grunted the hog again. "I understand now."

That night the hog gathered up all the young trees he could carry, and next morning took them over to the foot of the mountain where the monkey was waiting for him.

"Now," said the monkey, " I'll give you a few lessons in tree planting. First, dig a hole for each tree with your long snout. All the grubs and grass roots you find are yours."

The hog set to work and in two days he had the holes ready.

"Very good," said the monkey as he looked at the holes. "You are now ready for your second lesson. Take a tree and place its roots in a hole, then press the dirt well around the roots. Do the same with each tree and then you will be ready for the third lesson."

The hog did as he was told.

When the trees were all set out nicely, the monkey said: "Now, you must not let any weeds grow in our orchard; neither must you go far away while the trees are young, for some animal might come along and destroy them. I am going away for a month. Be careful to do as I have told you."

"Ugh, ugh," grunted the hog.

When the monkey returned, he found the trees growing nicely for Farmer Hog had cultivated them according to directions. However, as the hog had nothing to eat but grass roots and a few grubs he was nearly starved to death.

"Climb up one of the trees and toss down a few banana peelings," he said to the monkey.

"You surely do not expect to gather fruit from trees that have been in the ground for only a month," said the monkey. "It will be at least a year before I can promise you any peelings."

When the hog heard this he became angry, and called the monkey bad names; but when the monkey after a long time convinced him that it would be a year before the trees bore fruit, he was content to go about his work as usual.

In a year the trees began to bear fruit. Every day the monkey would climb to the top of a tree to eat bananas and to toss the peelings down to the faithful hog. The monkey grew fat. He invited some companions to share the fruit of the hog's labors with him, as he had much more than he could eat himself. Because the stupid old hog did not any know better, he was content to live upon the peelings, while he worked for others who enjoyed the real fruit.

MOKO AND TWELVE LITTLE EARTH MEN

Moko lived with his widowed aunt in a small hut on the side of a mountain that sloped toward a wide valley. His aunt was very poor, and had to work hard in the rice fields to support herself and her little nephew.

One time, the good woman became ill and was not able to work for several months. When their food was gone, she called Moko and told him to take a basket and go into the newly harvested fields, to see if he could find a little rice that the harvesters had left.

The little boy took the basket and went into the fields, but the gleaners had been there before him and gathered every head of the grain. He started home feeling very sad, for he and his aunt had but little to eat for a long time.

When he was nearly home, he noticed something white in the stubble in front of him. As he came near the object, he found that it was a beautiful white heron. The bird did not try to fly, so Moko walked to it, gently picked it up and placed it in his basket.

At first Moko was very happy, because he thought that he would take the bird home, and have his aunt cook it for their supper. He soon began to pity the bird, though, for he saw that its wing was broken.

As he was walking along with the bird under his arm, he suddenly heard a cry that seemed to come from the ground near his feet.

"Pull me out, pull me out," said a squeaky little voice.

Moko set his basket down and tried to find the place from which the voice came. Parting the grass carefully he soon saw the owner of the voice—a little earth man up to his middle in the mud.

Moko pulled the little fellow out and set him in a dry place. "Pull me out, pull me out," squeaked a second voice.

Moko again looked in the grass and found another earth man stuck in the mud as the first was. He pulled him out and stood him up by the other.

"Pull me out, pull me out," came a third voice. Moko pulled the third one out, but had scarcely done so when he heard more calls. One by one he drew the little fellows from the mud until he had pulled out twelve little earth men.

"Thank you for saving our lives," said the earth men all together. "It was a great big fellow with a great big foot who trod on us this afternoon, and when we begged him to pull us out of the mud he only laughed and passed on—but he'll be sorry, he'll be sorry," said all the little fellows as they disappeared in the stubble.

When Moko reached home, he told his aunt everything that had happened. "But," he said sorrowfully, "let's not kill the poor bird; its wing is broken, and it looks so gentle and sad. Perhaps we can find something else to eat tomorrow."

"You are very kind," said his aunt. "Take the heron and put it into the big box in the corner of the room. When its wing is well you may take it out into the fields again." Moko placed the bird in the box and went to bed.

Early next morning he ran to the box to see how his bird was. He raised the lid lightly, and what do you think he found? The box was full of clean, white rice, and the heron was sitting contentedly upon the grain. Moko and his aunt were now very happy. The good woman put some of the rice into a pot to cook. She then filled a bag with the grain and sent Moko to the market, where he sold it.

He bought some meat and fruit with the money. Every night the heron was placed in the box and every morning the box was full of rice.

A few weeks later Moko and his aunt rented a stall in the market of the town near their home to sell the rice. As the rice was of a fine quality, they had no trouble in selling all they could spare.

By the end of the year they had saved enough money to buy a small house in the town into which they moved.

Now Moko had a wicked old uncle whose name was Boonog. One night Boonog came to his relatives' home and asked them where they were getting so much rice to sell.

At first they would not tell him. Then the wicked man became angry and said that they were stealing the rice, and that he would have them thrown into jail.

Fearing that he would have to go to prison, Moko told his uncle about the bird.

"Let me see your rice-laying heron," Boonog demanded. When shown the bird he picked it up with the box and took it home with him.

Before going to bed Boonog went to the box where the bird was kept and said, "Now, lay rice for me as you have done for those poor relatives of mine, or else in the morning I shall chop off your head."

Early in the morning Boonog went to the box, expecting to find it full of rice, but instead it was full of small white stones.

He at once seized the heron and cut off its head. He then threw the dead bird out of the window.

A short time afterward Moko came to the home of his uncle and found the dead heron lying in the yard. He picked it up tenderly and carried it home.

In the ground just beneath his window he dug a hole. Here he buried the heron and stuck a sprig of an orange tree into the mound over the grave.

Next morning when Moko looked out of the window he saw a beautiful tree growing upon the grave, and around the tree were dancing the twelve little earth men whom he had pulled from the mud. They were dressed in green suits, with golden sashes, and gold helmets.

When they saw Moko, they smiled, took off their helmets to him, and disappeared in the grass. The little boy jumped out of bed as quickly as he could, and ran down stairs to look at the tree.

Far up near the top he saw growing a big, golden orange. He picked it and ran with it to his aunt. "This is indeed very strange," exclaimed the woman in great surprise. She examined the orange closely, but not being able to believe her own eyes, she took it to a goldsmith, who said it was the purest of gold and bought it at a great price.

Every morning the tree bore a golden orange, so the woman and her little nephew soon became rich. They had their old house torn down and a fine new home built in its place.

When Moko and his aunt moved into their new house, the cruel uncle came a second time and demanded to know where they had gotten so much money.

"This time I know you are stealing," he said, "and that you lied in the first place. Tell me the whole truth, or I shall have you arrested."

The woman and the boy were greatly frightened, so they told Boonog about the gold-bearing orange tree.

"Show me the tree," he demanded.

Moko pointed out the tree, and upon it were twelve large golden oranges, for they had not been gathered for twelve days.

The greedy man tore the beautiful shining oranges from the branches and hurried home with them. It was late in the evening, so he hid them in the box where he had kept the heron.

Before going to bed he was careful to fasten the lid with a padlock. Boonog could not sleep for thinking about the golden oranges.

Early in the morning he lighted a candle and went to open the box. As it was still dark, he had to place his face very near the lock in order to see the keyhole.

When he unlocked the box he peeped over the lid, but he had no sooner done so than out sprang the twelve little earth men.

They all caught him around the neck so tightly with their strong little arms that the big fellow tumbled as if dead.

"He'll be sorry, he'll be sorry," said the little men. "He not only trampled us into the mud with his big foot, but robbed the kind little boy and the poor widow."

While Boonog lay upon the floor, one of the earth men took him by his nose and stretched it out till it was a yard long.

One took him by the big toes, pulling them out as long as his nose. They pulled out his ears until they looked like donkeys' ears. They then pulled him up by his fingers.

As they did so his fingers stretched out until they were almost as long as his big toes.

Boonog scrambled to his feet and tried to catch the earth men but the twelve little fellows had enough fun, so they hopped out of the window and were never seen again. Boonog then poked around in the box with his long fingers trying to find the gold, but he found nothing but a lot of sticky mud from the rice field.

When the wicked fellow's wife and children got up in the morning and saw this strange-looking man, they ran screaming to the street. Their cries attracted all the neighbors, who came as fast as they could to see what was the matter.

When they saw Boonog with his long nose, his donkeys' ears, and his long fingers they ran home to bar their windows and doors—indeed, such a sight was enough to frighten anyone.

In a week or two all the women of the town called upon the mayor to ask him to put the terrible-looking man away where he could not be seen.

The mayor looked wise but said that he could not do anything. The women then took things in their own hands. One evening they came with sticks, and chased the ugly man into the forest.

After seeking in vain for a whole year for some human being to be his friend, Boonog at last tried to make friends with the hogs, but even they would have nothing to do with him.

At the first sight of him they scampered into the brush as fast as their legs could take them. The wife and children of Boonog would have starved to death had it not been for the kindness of Moko, who took care of them. Moko even furnished food for his uncle by placing it upon a stump at the edge of the forest where Boonog could come at night to get it.

Boonog had been so badly punished for his meanness that after a few years, when his face straightened out and his fingers and toes grew short again, he came back to his family and lived a kinder life ever after.

MR. MONK AND MR. TOWSER DOG

A dog and a monkey met at a spring where they had come for a drink.

“Good morning, Mr. Towser,” said the monkey.

“Good morning, Mr. Monk,” said the dog, for he knew that this was the wise old monkey whom all the forest people called Mr. Monk.

“How goes it with you, Mr. Towser?” asked the monkey.

“Oh,” replied Towser, “I could not complain if it were not for these pesky fleas; I really believe there are a million on my back now. They make my life miserable. How goes it with you, may I ask?”

“I have nothing to complain of,” replied the monkey, “except the shortage of the banana crop. I am thinking of going to the other side of the mountain where they say bananas are plentiful, but I am such a poor walker that I dislike very much to undertake the trip.”

“Do the fleas ever bother you? “ asked the dog.

“Not to speak of,” replied the monkey. “Sometimes a few get on my back, but I soon pick them off.”

“I shall make a bargain with you,” said the dog.

“What is it? “ asked the monkey.

“If you will pick off my fleas,” replied the dog, “you may climb upon my back and I shall carry you to the other side of the mountain. You know I am swift of foot, and I can take you over there in a short time.”

“Agreed,” said the monkey.

The dog then lay down in a cool, damp place under a tree. and the monkey began to pick off the fleas. In less than an hour he had gotten them all.

"Get up, now! Let's be going," said the monkey.

The dog was so sound asleep that the monkey could not awaken him. All that night and part of the next day the dog slept. When he did wake up, he yawned and said: "My, how hungry I am! I must find something to eat at once."

"When are you going to take me to the other side of the mountain?" asked the monkey.

"Who are you? " snarled the dog.

"I am the fellow that picked the fleas off your back," said the monkey, greatly surprised at the way the dog acted.

"Well, you may have the fleas for your trouble," replied the ungrateful dog, as he trotted off.

A month later the dog came back to the spring, where he met the monkey again.

"How do you do, Mr. Monk? " he asked, trying to be polite.

"I can't complain," replied the monkey rather coldly, "and how are you, Towser?"

"Same old trouble," replied the dog. "I do believe my fleas are worse than they were the other time I met you."

The monkey said nothing. The dog sat down and began to bite and scratch at the fleas. After a while he said: "Mr. Monk, that was a mean trick I played you last month, but I am sorry, and I promise you that it will never happen again. Just rid me of these pests and I will carry you to the other side of the mountain in less time than it will take to pick them off."

" I am sorry, Mr. Towser," replied the monkey. "I have made up my mind to stay here. But," he continued, " there are a number of crabs down near the mouth of the river who told me a short time ago that they would like to see the other side of the mountain. Perhaps you can make a bargain with them. Crabs have excellent claws, which are said to be fine for catching fleas."

"Show me the crabs," said the dog.

The monkey led him to the crabs.

The dog lay down and said to the monkey, "Tell them to pick off my fleas in a hurry, and I'll carry all the crabs in the river's mouth to the other side of the mountain."

The crabs gathered around the dog. The monkey whispered in an old crab's ear. The old crab stood up and made a little speech.

after which all the crabs began to sharpen their pincers. About a hundred of them then crawled upon the dog, some on his back, some on his legs, and others upon his neck.

The monkey then stood at one side and said to them in the crab language, "When I count three and say the word 'go' it is time for work."

No sooner had the monkey counted three and uttered the word "go" than all the crabs began to pinch the dog unmercifully.

"Ki, Yi!" yelped Towser. "Bow, wow," he barked as he rolled over and over in the sand and snapped at the crabs. "For goodness' sake," he said to the monkey, "tell these terrible things to stop."

"Are they not picking off your fleas?" asked the monkey.

"They may be," yelped the dog, "but they are taking off my skin with the fleas."

The monkey then spoke to the crabs, after which he said to Towser: "The crabs say they agreed to pick off all your fleas if you would carry them over the mountain. They are doing it, and now they cannot understand why you dance around and yelp, unless it is because you are so happy. Be still for an hour and they will have finished."

"Tell them to stop now, and I will take them to the other side of the mountain, right away," howled the dog.

"The crabs say," replied the monkey, "that they want me to go along so that I can tell them when they reach the other side of the mountain. Crabs are stupid things, you know, and cannot understand the dog language."

"Hop on, and be quick about it!" yelped the dog.

The monkey then climbed upon the dog's back and the dog began to run as fast as he could. When Towser reached the place where the monkey wanted to go, the monkey jumped off his back and rolled over with laughter.

"Say, friend Towser," he said, "the crabs do not like the scenery over here, and they want you to take them back home at once."

The dog tucked his tail between his legs and ran all the way back to the mouth of the river. Here the crabs let go and tumbled into the water.

Mr. Towser was always careful after that to keep the bargains he made.

THE BUFFALOES AND THE HERONS

The heron is in this story the familiar "buffalo bird," which associates with the native carabao, or water buffalo. One often sees a dozen or more of these birds perched upon the back of one of these huge animals.

The water buffaloes and the herons, as everyone who has lived in the Philippines knows, are the greatest of friends. Wherever one sees a buffalo grazing, there is at least one heron near him. Often a dozen or more of the birds may be seen perched upon the broad back of the huge animal, and sometimes two or three will light upon his head. No buffalo would think of injuring a heron; neither would a heron do anything that would annoy his friend.

There was a time, long ago, when the two were enemies. This was due to the fact that the home of each is in the marshes. The buffaloes said that all the marshes, by right, belonged to them; but the herons claimed that the marshes were theirs. On this account there was a continual quarrel between the big, ugly animals and the pretty, white birds. Whenever a flock of herons lighted in the marshes to look for food, the buffaloes would shake their heads and run bellowing at them to scare them away. Sometimes a big foot would crush one of the birds deep into the mud. The herons also did everything that they could to worry the buffaloes. They would splash mud all over the marsh grass as they waded about looking for frogs and snails, and if a buffalo happened to be sleeping, they would swoop down from above and try to pierce his eyes with their sharp-bills.

One time a wise old heron said to his companions: "There's really no reason for all this trouble. There's plenty of room in the marshes for both of us. Let us try to make peace with the buffaloes."

"Good," said the rest of the herons.

The old heron went at once to see the buffaloes about making peace with them, but the buffaloes told him that there would be no peace unless all the herons would leave the marshes.

"Well," said the wise old bird to himself as he flew back to his companions, "I shall have to depend upon my wits to make peace with the stubborn buffaloes."

Not long afteward a big, old buffalo was sleeping at the edge of the marsh when a large cowfly lit upon his back and stung him. The buffalo at once began to dream that he was hitched to a plow, and that his master had stuck a sharp stick in his back. He jumped up and ran bellowing through the field, thinking that the stick was fast in his back, and that he was dragging the plow after him.

The wise old heron upon seeing the buffalo, lit upon his back, caught the fly and swallowed it.

The buffalo at once stopped, and asked the heron, "How were you able to draw that sharp stick from my back—and what did you do with it?

"Oh," replied the heron, "I drew it out with this strong bill of mine, and then I swallowed it."

"Who would have thought you could do such a thing," said the buffalo. "Pray tell me where the plow is that I was dragging."

"I swallowed that, too," replied the heron.

"Where, where, then is my master?" asked the buffalo.

"He's with the stick and the plow," said the heron.

The buffalo ran as fast as he could to the herd and told what the heron had done. All the animals except two believed the story, and advised making peace with the herons at once, for they thought that the heron was the strongest of birds, since it was able

The old heron went at once to see the buffaloes

to swallow a man and a plow.

Now the two buffaloes that did not believe the story were old Nooang, the ruler of the herd, and Club Tail.

Not long after this, Club Tail was taking a bath in a mudhole. He was all covered but his nose, when all at once a frog crawled into his ear and was stuck fast. The frog began to kick with all his might, and to croak at the same time. Club Tail jumped out of the mudhole, and ran away bellowing at the top of his voice. As he was big and heavy it was not long before his breath gave out, and he fell down upon the ground.

The wise heron, seeing the buffalo, flew down from a tamarind tree and asked what was the matter.

"Oh," bellowed Club Tail, "there's a cane mill with a zebu hitched to it in my ear. I can hear the creaking of the rollers, and feel the sharp hoofs of the zebu as he goes round and round, hitched to the long sweep of the mill. Please, will you not get the cane mill and the ox out of my ear? If you cannot do something at once my head will surely burst."

"Turn over on your side," said the heron, "and let me look into your ear."

Club Tail turned over, and the heron put his bill into the ear, drew out the frog, and swallowed it.

Club Tail scrambled to his feet just in time to see the heron crook his neck as the frog went down into his crop.

"Where in the world are the cane mill and the ox? " he asked.

"Stupid one," replied the heron, "they went the way of the man and the plow."

The big animal ran as fast as he could to his companions and told everyone that he had seen with his own eyes the heron swallow a cane mill and a large zebu.

All except old Nooang believed the story, and wanted to make peace that very day with the herons. "If," they said, "a heron can swallow a cane mill and a zebu, what is to keep him from swallowing one of us?"

"Nonsense," replied Nooang, "you are foolish to believe such things."

Not long after that the farmers, wishing to drain the marsh, dug a ditch in order to let the water run off. The buffaloes wondered what they would do without water, and feared they would have to move away in order to find drink and mudholes in which to bathe. Of all the buffaloes, Nooang took the matter to heart more than any of the others.

One evening Nooang saw a large flock of herons around a pool near the middle of the marsh. Going up to them he noticed that they were all drinking. He stood still to hear what the herons had to say.

"Well," said the wise old heron, "we have just about drunk the swamp dry, and we shall have to fly over to the other side of the mountain before long to find more water. Of course we did not need so much water, but we had to drink it up just to get rid of those stubborn buffaloes. When they are gone, we shall come back again, and have all the marsh to ourselves."

Upon hearing this, Nooang ran as fast as he could, and called all the buffaloes together.

"Oh," he bellowed, "the herons are drinking the swamp dry. Let us make peace with them at once."

The buffaloes then went to the herons and made an agreement to live in peace with them, and to share the marshes on equal terms.

So the buffaloes and the herons ever afterward lived together in peace and happiness.

THE THREE MAGICIANS

Once there lived three wise magicians whose names were Akbar, Regan, and Goobat. Each claimed that he was able to perform a more wonderful trick than the others, and for that reason the three men frequently quarreled among themselves.

One day the magicians met in the market place, and forthwith began a dispute. Pretty soon they came to blows.

Now it happened that a rug weaver, a saddler, and a milk peddler, in passing by, saw the fighting, and stepped aside to separate the contestants.

"What business have you fellows to meddle in this argument of ours?" said the magicians. "Go away and leave us alone."

"Come," said the rug weaver, the saddler, and the milk peddler, "what's the use of fighting? Let each of you perform a trick and we shall judge which is the most wonderful. We assure you, gentlemen, that we shall act with the greatest fairness."

"Very well," said Akbar to the weaver, "bring me one of your finest rugs."

"Fair enough," said Regan to the saddler, "bring me one of your finest saddles."

"All right," said Goobat to the milkman, "bring me your jar of milk."

The weaver brought his rug, the saddler his saddle, and the milk peddler his jar of milk.

Akbar took the rug, said over it some magical words, and the rug became a piece of flat dough. He then made a fire and baked the dough into bread of a nice brown color.

"Wonderful!" said the judges.

Regan took the saddle, said over it some magical words, and the saddle became a ray fish. He then roasted the fish until it was tender.

"Wonderful!" said the judges.

Goobat now took the milk jar, said over it some magical words, and the milk became red wine.

"Wonderful!" said the judges.

"Well," said the magicians to the judges, "you have seen what we have done; now tell us which of the three tricks was the most wonderful."

The judges withdrew to a, corner of the market place, where they sat down to think the matter over. In an hour or two they came back, and said:

"Sirs, this is too difficult a question for us to decide. Let's bring the matter before the Caji, who is skilled in the business of judging."

So they all went to the Caji and asked him to decide the question.

The Caji tasted the bread. "Excellent!" said he. "Pass me the fish."

He tasted the fish. "Excellent! " said he. "Pass me the wine."

He took a long swig from the jar.

"Excellent!" said he, smacking his lips.

"Gentlemen," said the Caji, after he had sampled the food and drink, "I never tasted better bread, better fish, or better wine, but I can't tell for the life of me whether it is a greater trick to turn a rug into bread, a saddle into a fish, or milk into wine. For my trouble," continued the Caji, "I shall keep all these articles for myself. Good day."

Upon hearing what the Caji had to say, the magicians walked out.

The rug weaver, the saddler, and the milk peddler ran after them, demanding pay for their wares. The magicians escaped through the crowd, however, and the three men, who had volunteered to act as peacemakers, went home, sadder and wiser men.

MR. MONK AND KING TUMBO

Old Tumbo, the elephant, was a mighty king. He ruled not only over the elephants, but over all the other animals as well.

One time the animals met to honor their king.

"Great is our Tumbo!" they cried. "He is the king of all the jungle. He fears no animal, large or small."

Tumbo stood upon a high place in an opening in the forest. He had thrown back his huge ears in order to catch the words of praise from the other animals, and his little eyes fairly sparkled when he saw a great lion with a shaggy mane bowing low to him. As he looked around and saw the faces of all the other animals turned towards him, he said to himself:

"What they say about me is indeed true. I am great. I am king of all the jungle. I fear no animal, large or small."

Now it seems that a hungry cat had seen a timid little mouse among the other animals. She stole forward. Now the bright eyes of the little mouse saw her, and ran under the end of Tumbo's trunk which was only a couple of inches above the ground. She saw the opening at the end and just as the cat reached out a paw, she darted into it.

The instant Tumbo felt the mouse inside his trunk, he gave a mighty roar and began to run as fast as he could. Seeing their king so badly frightened, the rest of the animals tumbled over one another in their haste to get back to the jungle.

At length the elephants formed themselves in a circle around their king to keep him from running any farther. Tumbo threw himself upon the ground, rolled over, and bellowed:

"Help me! Get him out! Get him out! He is killing me; he is killing me."

"Get out what—and where is he?" asked the other elephants.

"The mouse, the mouse," cried Tumbo, "he's inside my trunk."

Just then the elephants heard the squeaky voice of Mr. Monk calling from the top of a palm tree:

"What is the matter with our brave King Tumbo?"

"Well," said the monkey, as he scratched his head, "I suppose I shall have to pull him out. Lie down on your back and let me look into your trunk."

Tumbo lay down on his back and the monkey put one eye close to the end of his trunk.

"Can you see him?" asked Tumbo.

"Yes," replied the monkey.

"Where is he? " asked Tumbo.

"Halfway up," answered the monkey.

"Pull him out," begged Tumbo, "and hurry about it."

The monkey put his hand into the end of the elephant's trunk to reach the mouse, but Tumbo jumped to his feet and once more began to run as fast as he could, bellowing to the other elephants:

"Oh, it is bad enough to have a mouse in one's trunk, but much worse to have a monkey. The monkey's hand has been halfway up my trunk."

"Well," said Mr. Monk to the elephants as they began to gather around him, "there is but one thing to do if you wish me to get the mouse. You will have to hold your king fast while I put my arm in his trunk."

"We shall hold him," said the elephants.

A half dozen big fellows then caught Tumbo and threw him to the ground. Two held his hind legs, two held his front legs, one held his tail, and another sat upon his side.

"Oh! Oh! Oh!" wept Tumbo as the monkey put his arm up his trunk, "please do not let the monkey crawl up my trunk."

But he had hardly said this, when the monkey drew out his hand with the little, trembling mouse in it.

Tumbo scrambled to his feet and trumpeted joyfully. The elephants thanked the monkey; then in a body went back to their forest home. But the news soon spread among all the elephants throughout the jungle that a mouse had run into their king's trunk, and ever since that day the elephants have been afraid of mice.

MR. MONK AND THE NOISY GECKO

The Philippine gecko is a very large, noisy lizard. He sometimes crawls into the hollow endings of bamboo rafters, and disturbs sleepers with his cry. It is a fact that he utters his cry seven times before stopping. He is a perfectly harmless animal, though somewhat hideous to behold. The gecko is not to be confounded with the little wall lizard, or *butiki.* This little animal comes out upon the inner walls of houses at night, in order to catch moths and other insects that are attracted by the light. One can see several hundred of them in one house. The natives never harm the *butikis,* but they rout the *geckos* on account of their music.

Once upon a time a noisy gecko moved into that part of the woods where the songbirds lived. As the birds had always been used to good music, they did not like their new neighbor from the start; for a gecko is a big quarrelsome lizard with a hoarse, froglike voice. The one in this story was as large as a young alligator, and his voice was louder and hoarser than that of any bullfrog you ever heard. Whenever he caught a bug, or any other kind of insect, he would crawl backward into a dry, hollow limb, which served him for a home, as well as a sounding box for his voice. Here he would cry "geck-o" seven times. Now, if he caught a hundred insects in one day he would utter his cry seven hundred times; but the truth of the matter was, he often caught a thousand. So you can see he kept the woods resounding at all times of the day with his terrible croaking.

"This will never do," said the birds. "We cannot put up with the harsh voice of that fellow. We scarcely get our throats tuned for a chorus before he spoils everything with his dreadful notes."

"It's too bad," warbled a little canary sadly, "and to make matters worse, he's teaching our young ones to like poor music. Oh, I can't bear the thought!" she went on. "It was only this morning that I heard a flock of our dear little yellowbills imitating the lizard."

"Suppose we ask him to leave," said an old warbler. "But in order not to appear too unneighborly, let's first offer him a present of some insects."

"That's a fine idea," chirped the songbirds. So they caught a lot of choice insects and took them over to the lizard, whom they found sunning himself on the side of his limb.

"Good morning, neighbor," sang out the canary in her sweetest tones. "We thought you might be hungry, so we brought you a lot of nice bugs which we caught farther down the river—where they are most plentiful."

"Thanks," gurgled the lizard. "For your kindness, I shall entertain you with some of my best music."

When he had swallowed a big fuzzy caterpillar, the first insect offered him, he puffed out his sides and uttered his song fourteen times, croaking it in deeper tones than he had ever croaked it before.

The terrible cry so shocked the poor little canary bird that she fell over in a swoon, and had to be carried home.

With each insect the gecko repeated his song, but when he had swallowed the last bug, only the old warbler had stayed to listen, for the other songbirds had flown away in fear and disgust.

"We have noticed that the bugs seem to make you happy," said the old warbler, rather nervously, at the close of the meal. "So we came to tell you that there are all kinds of insects farther down the river. We are sure that you would like it better there."

"What you say about the insects is true," replied the gecko, "but the climate is damp and I fear it would injure my voice. I have made up my mind to keep my home here. Within a short time," continued the lizard, "I expect to send for my wife and seven grown sons. When they arrive, I promise you some real music, the like of which was never heard in all this neighborhood. In the meantime should you wish to hear me sing again, just bring some more insects and I shall be glad to entertain you."

The gecko then slid into his hollow branch and went to sleep.

The warbler flew home, and in sad tones told his companions what the lizard had told him. After they had heard the story, the songbirds thought the best thing to do would be to move away where they would no longer be compelled to listen to the croaking of the gecko. This they were very sorry to do, for their grandfathers and grandmothers had been hatched in nests built in the old, old trees that they were now preparing to leave, perhaps never to see them again.

The next morning as they hopped sadly about among the branches, a wise old monkey came swinging through the tree tops.

"What's the trouble?" he asked. "You folks are singing the most doleful songs I ever heard."

"Oh," replied the canary pitifully, "it's all on account of that awful lizard. His voice is driving us crazy, so we are going away where we can't hear him."

"Have you asked him to leave? " inquired the monkey.

"We suggested it." answered the birds, "but he said he was going to stay. Furthermore, he is going to send for his family in a few days."

"Remain here in peace, you silly things," said the monkey when he saw how badly the birds felt about the matter. "I'll see to it that your noisy neighbor does not bother you much longer."

"Thank you,' chirped the birds, "but we are afraid that you cannot do anything with him. He's very stubborn."

"I've dealt with fellows far more stubborn than the gecko," replied the monkey, laughing.

The songbirds flew back to their customary places, while the monkey swung from limb to limb until he came to the tree in which the gecko lived. The lizard, an hour or two before, had feasted upon some bugs that he found sucking the juice from a wild gourdvine, and at the time of the monkey's arrival, was taking his customary noonday nap at the bottom of the hollow limb.

The monkey peeped into the hole and called out:

"Wake up, neighbor; I've come to see you on an important matter and cannot wait until you finish your nap."

"Get away from here!" croaked the lizard. "What do you mean by disturbing my rest? What do you want, anyway?" he gurgled as he crawled out of his hole.

"I just came to tell you," said the monkey, "that your voice is worrying the poor songbirds out of their wits. I suggest that you move over to that part of the woods where the crows, hoot owls parrots, frogs, and other squawking things live. They tell me that they are in great need of a bass, as the principal bullfrog singer is sick. I am sure you could take his place admirably. You'll find a nice, hollow limb over there, and the trees fairly swarm with bugs."

"Begone!" croaked the stubborn animal as he swelled out his throat and wiggled his tail. "Those ungrateful birds shall not get rid of me. Just wait till my family comes; then the birds will have some real cause to grumble."

Next day about noon the monkey saw a wasps' nest hanging on a twig near the top of the gecko's tree. This he broke off carefully, so as to not disturb the insects, and holding it at arm's length, slid down to the hollow limb. He then dropped the wasps upon the lizard's head, then sprang aside and hid himself among the leaves.

To the great surprise of the monkey, the gecko shot out his long hard tongue and licked in the wasps, one after another, bellowing his usual cry at each gulp. He then came out of his hole to look for more wasps. On seeing the monkey, he said:

"A whole nest of nice little brown bugs fell into my hollow limb a moment ago. Do you see any more of them over there?" he continued, licking his lips.

"No," answered the monkey, greatly puzzled.

Scratching his head vigorously in an effort to stir up a thought, the monkey at length asked, "What kind of bug do you really like best of all?"

"Beetles—the big, black, snapping kind," replied the gecko. "I wonder if you could tell me where I could find a few of them."

"Yes, I can," answered the monkey. "Tomorrow morning you'll find half a dozen big ones on the limb over yonder," he continued, pointing to the place, "but you'll have to be up early, because they always fly off at sunrise."

"I'll be up early," gurgled the lizard in reply. The monkey searched the forest until he found a large chewing-gum tree, with a nice ball of sticky gum oozing from the bark. From the gum he molded what looked like six large snapping beetles, then rolled them in some black dust to give them a coating, and late that night placed them in a row upon the limb that he had shown to the lizard.

Upon waking at early daybreak, the gecko poked his head out of his hole and dimly saw the six large gum beetles.

"Yum, yum—snapping bugs," he said to himself. "What a fine breakfast I'm going to have!"

Slipping up to the gum beetles, he shot out his tongue and raked in the one nearest him. He then pounced upon the next, then the next, until he had all six of them in his mouth at one time. He was so excited over the bugs that he tried to gulp them all down and say "geck-o" as he did it. This only made the warmed mass of gum stick to his lips, tongue, and nose. As he could not swallow the gum he let go and fell off the limb into the sand, where he tried to dig the sticky stuff out of his mouth with his claws.

Up went a fore foot, but it stuck fast in his mouth. Up went the other, and it stuck like the first one. Then went up a hind foot, and it promptly stuck like the others. He then gave a mighty flop with his tail, driving the sharp, scaly end of it between his jaws. It, too, stuck fast. The lizard now stiffened himself into a big ring, like a hoop, and begun to roll around in the sand.

The monkey came down from a tree, from which he had all the time been watching, and picked up a stick. With one hand he took hold of the gecko, and with the other rapped him with the stick, just as a boy does when he is rolling a hoop. This sent the lizard forward at great speed. To help matters along, every time he rolled around, the lizard hit the ground with his free foot. Away he rolled through the woods, across the valleys, and over the hills, while the foot went pit-a-pat, pit-a-pat, pit-a-pat every time he made a circle—and if he has not rolled down where the hoot owls and parrots live, he is still rolling.

THE MAN OF THE WOODS AND THE GIANT

There once lived a great, ugly, giant in a castle near a lake. His name was Ampong. Every day he would go into the forest and catch an animal, which he roasted for his dinner.

One time the animals held a meeting to see what they could do to get rid of the giant. To this meeting, there came all kinds of creatures, both large and small.

An old orangutan, who had once belonged to a sailor, and who was known throughout the jungle for his great wisdom, was chosen to be the leader. The orangutan was called "The Man of the Woods."

When the meeting had come to order, The Man of the Woods asked the different creatures what they could do to help get rid of the giant.

"What can you do, Brother Buffalo?" he asked.

"I can bellow at him," said the buffalo.

"What can you do, Brother Turtle?"

"I can bite him," said the turtle.

"What can you do, Nest of Hornets?"

"We can sting him," said the hornets.

"What can you do, Brother Boa?"

"I can squeeze him," said the boa.

"What can you do, Brother Crocodile?"

"I can eat him up," said the crocodile.

All the other creatures were asked what they could do, and nearly everyone said he could do something to help. The Man of the Woods, however, decided to choose as his helpers the buffalo, the turtle, the hornets, the boa, and the crocodile.

"Are you all willing to do what I tell you?" he asked. "Yes," bellowed the buffalo.

"Yes," snapped the turtle.

"Yes," buzzed the hornets.

"Yes," hissed the boa.

"Yes," croaked the crocodile.

"Come with me, then," said The Man of the Woods. "Let's go to Ampong's castle. Only do as I tell you, and all will be well."

While all the other animals went back to their homes, The Man of the Woods, the buffalo, the turtle, the hornets, the boa, and the crocodile set out for Ampong's castle. When they arrived in the neighborhood where Ampong lived, they hid in the bushes and waited until they saw him leave his castle. When he was out of sight, they all hurried forward. The Man of the Woods, the buffalo, and the turtle went in and barred all the doors and windows. The hornets built themselves a big, bell-shaped nest near the top of a tree in the yard. The boa coiled himself around a limb of the tree, while the crocodile went to the lake.

About nightfall they heard the heavy footsteps of Ampong on the stone flags of the courtyard. When he tried to open the door and found it locked and barred, he became furiously angry.

"Open this door! " he roared, " or I'll eat alive whoever is in my house."

The Man of the Woods, who had crawled through a little window up near the roof and sat perched upon a window sill out of the giant's reach, said:

"Ampong, a great king is passing through this country and he has decided to rest here a few days. He does not care to be disturbed. Kindly withdraw to a distance."

"And pray, who are you to dare give me such a message? " demanded Ampong.

"I am the king's clown," said The Man of the Woods.

"Tell your king to be gone at once or else I'll break all his bones," roared the giant.

"Save your breath, Mr. Ampong," said The Man of the Woods. "My king is a mightier giant than you. Just put your ear to the keyhole and he will perhaps whisper something that will interest you."

Ampong, who was very stupid and very curious, put his ear to the keyhole. The buffalo, which stood with his mouth near the keyhole, bellowed so loud that Ampong clapped his hands

When Ampong was out of sight they all hurried forward

over his ears, and ran away as fast as his legs would carry him. He finally stopped in the shade of a tree to get his breath. Scratching his head, he said to himself, "If that's only a whisper, then the king must indeed be a most powerful giant. Maybe I had better keep away for a while."

Ampong wandered about in the woods for several days. As he was lazy and liked to sleep a great deal, he longed to be back in his soft bed where he could rest easily, and one day about noon he went back to his castle, determined to turn the strange king out.

Now the turtle was sunning himself upon the stone steps.

"What is this?" Ampong asked of the clown who had seen him approaching and had again seated himself on the window-sill.

"Oh, that is just one of our little ants who, no doubt, fell from the sole of the king's boot," answered the Man of the Woods.

"Well," thought Ampong as he again scratched his thick head, "if the king is able to carry around ants like that he must indeed be king of a mighty country."

Ampong reached down to pick up the ant to examine it, but no sooner had he laid his hands upon it than snap! went the turtle's strong jaws upon his thumb.

Away the giant ran, with the turtle hanging to his thumb He roared so loud that he made the forest resound with his bellowing. As he ran the turtle let go, but the giant was so frightened that he did not stop running until he reached the middle of a large swamp, and there he stayed and nursed his sore finger.

But in a day or two Ampong began to long for his bed again, especially as the mosquitoes and other swamp insects stung him so badly that he could scarcely sleep a wink. So one morning he again stole back to his castle, hoping that the "king" and his party had left. He found that the door was still barred, and was informed by The Man of the Woods from his high seat on the sill that the king was still asleep and must not be disturbed. Ampong sat down to think of something to do. His eyes fell on the hornet's nest.

"What's that' he asked curiously.

"That's the king's dinner bell," answered The Man of the Woods, "but be careful not to ring it or you'll wake the king."

"That's just what I want to do," said Ampong. "Then we'll fight it out. I'll show him who is master of this castle."

The stupid giant saw a vine hanging from the tree and thought it was the rope to ring the bell. He took hold of it and gave it a mighty jerk. This woke up the hornets, who flew down and stung him on the face, lips, nose, eyes, and ears.

Away he went to the woods again, clawing about his head and bellowing at the top of his voice. At last he came to a river, and jumped head over heels into the water in order to free himself of the terrible creatures.

Now it would seem by this time that Ampong ought to have known enough to keep away from the castle forever, but he was very, very stupid, and could not remember anything very long, except that his bed was very comfortable.

"Oh, my bed, my soft bed," he groaned one night as he rolled upon the hard earth where he was trying to sleep. "Tomorrow I am surely going back to turn that fellow out."

Now it happened that when Ampong returned the fourth time the first thing he saw was the boa, who had selected a very conspicuous limb on which to place himself.

"What is this thing?" he asked the "clown," who was waiting for him.

"That's the king's belt," said The Man of the Woods. "It is a fine one set with two big diamonds, so be careful that you do not touch it."

Just to show what he thought of "the clown's" king, Ampong seized the "belt" and tried to buckle it around his body. The boa at once began to squeeze him with all his strength. Ampong fell upon the hard ground, and rolled over and over, until the boa finally loosened itself, but Ampong was so scared that he fled away again. His ribs ached badly, and he became angrier than ever. He spent hours planning what he would do. When morning came he was on his way to the castle. As he passed the lake he saw the crocodile lying motionless on the surface of the water.

"What is that?" he said aloud, and coming to a halt.

"That's the king's pleasure boat," said the Man of the Woods, who this time was in a tree nearby. "The king does not allow anyone to ride in it but himself," he added as Ampong went closer to the edge of the water.

"Well, I'm going to ride in it," said the stupid giant as he stepped upon the broad back of the crocodile, who at once swam quietly but quickly away. When he came to the middle of the lake, he gave a sudden jerk to his tail and flung Ampong into the water. Then the crocodile caught him with his strong jaws, and that was the end of him.

When the animals of the jungle heard the glad news there was much rejoicing. A great feast was spread in honor of The Man of the Woods and his helpers for what they had done to make jungle life happy once more.

MR. MONK AND THE SMART YOUNG LION

A long time ago the jungle people met to choose a new king. Tumbo, the elephant, had been king for so long that no one could remember when he began to rule. Although the forest people thought a great deal of their old king, they knew that he was growing childish. On that account he could not be depended upon in time of danger. In fact, Tumbo had asked his subjects to elect another king, for he knew that he was not able to rule any more, especially since a mouse had scared him so badly by climbing up the inside of his trunk.

So he called all the animals together and spoke to them.

"Beloved subjects," he began, "I have been your king for a long, long time, so long that I have grown old in your service. Though bowed down with the weight of years, I truly hope that many moons may yet come and go, before it is time for me to begin my journey to the other land. But I feel that now there is one among you who is more capable of being your king than I. I therefore—Goodness! " bellowed the old elephant in the middle of his speech, "I do believe I saw that pesky mouse!"

It was with some difficulty that the animals could get Tumbo to believe that he had not seen a mouse. In a little while he became calm, but before he went on with his talk he commanded all the mice to withdraw to the outer edge of the circle of animals. To make sure that they did so he ordered all the cats to see that his commands were obeyed.

"As I was saying," he then went on, "there is one among you who is better fitted to be your king than I. I therefore give up in his favor. All of you know the wise monkey, who has been my constant friend and helper ever since he did me the great favor of pulling the mouse from my trunk. Some of you may think that the monkey, because of his small size, is not the one to be selected as your ruler, but what you need in a king is not size, but brains. Let his wisdom guide you. Should he need any big fellows like myself and Brother Hippo to help him carry out his plans, he has but to call upon us."

Tumbo then lifted the monkey with his trunk far above his head, where all the animals could see him.

"Bravo! He shall be our king! " shouted nearly all the animals together.

"Talk the matter over among yourselves," said Tumbo, "then go on with the election." Now, a smart young lion, with a long mane and a very long tail, had come to the meeting, hoping that he would be chosen king. His great-great-great-grandfather had been king before Tumbo. For that reason he said the kingship rightfully belonged to him, but to tell the truth, it was his beautiful mane and tail more than anything else that made him think he ought to be elected.

So the young lion stalked about among the animals, asking that they vote for him. From what they said, he felt sure that he would be elected, and assumed quite a royal air.

However, when the votes had been counted, it was found that the monkey had been elected by a big majority. The new king at once stood on a stump and made a speech in which he thanked everyone for electing him, and promised that he would do his best to be a wise and just king. Tumbo then placed a crown of leaves upon his head, and the animals made the forest resound with their cheers.

All this time the disappointed young lion lay in the grass and beat the ground with his long tail. Just as the monkey king hopped off the stump, the lion suddenly uttered a mighty roar and sprang toward him. Had it not been for the quickness of the monkey, the animals would have had to elect another king.

When Tumbo saw what had happened, he ran bellowing at the lion and would have fought with him at once. But the monkey sprang upon the elephant's head and whispered something in his ear.

The proud lion stood upon the stump, arched his back, and lashed his tail, greatly to the amusement of his so-called friends, the jackals and the hyenas.

The meeting broke up in disorder. Tumbo, the new king, the monkey, and a big, old hippo withdrew to a dark place in the woods to talk things over.

"Do as he tells you," said Tumbo to the hippo at the end of the secret conference, "and the smart young lion will soon steal off into the mountains where nobody will see him again."

"You can depend upon me," grunted the hippo, with a great smile such as only a hippo can make.

The three animals searched the forest until they found a great hole in the ground at the root of a huge tree.

"Back in here," said the monkey to the hippo, "so that we can try out our plan."

The hippo backed into the hole until only his head remained above the ground. He then opened his huge mouth, letting his lower jaw rest on a level with the surface, while his upper jaw stood up like the back of a chair.

"What a fine throne!" exclaimed the monkey. "It is leather-bound, lined with red plush, set with two big diamonds, and inlaid with ivory. How the lion will envy me when he sees me sitting on this throne!"

He now hopped upon the hippo's broad tongue, and the "throne" turned around! He then jumped upon the hippo's nose, and the "throne" closed; then he jumped to the ground and the throne disappeared.

A week later the monkey sent a call throughout the jungle for the animals to come together.

When the lion saw the monkey king sitting upon the beautiful new "throne," he again lay down, gnashed his teeth, and beat the ground with his tail. Then stealing up close to the monkey, he gave a spring and landed right in the hippo's big mouth, as the monkey leaped nimbly to one side.

"What a fine throne!" exclaimed the monkey to the Hippo

Sitting upon the great lower jaw of the hippo, the lion uttered another mighty roar, then told the animals that he was their true king even though they had not elected him. His great eyes shone so terribly that it was all the monkey could do to keep the animals from running away into the jungle.

The monkey now slipped up to the hippo's ear and whispered: "'Tis time. 'Tis time."

Snap! Went the hippo's strong jaws, and they closed like a vice upon the lion's tail.

Immediately there was such a roar as had never before been heard in all the jungle, but roar and scratch as he might, the lion could not get free from the powerful jaws.

Tighter, tighter, closed the jaws upon the lion's tail, until they bit it off close to the lion's body.

"Oh, my beautiful tail!" cried the lion as he sprang forward and disappeared into the dark woods.

The animals were never bothered after that by the smart young lion, for with his tail gone, he had no more claim to be king. He was so ashamed of himself that he sneaked off into the mountains, and never showed himself again.

The monkey, who from then on was known as King Amuy the First, hung the lion's tail on a limb above his throne. It is said the old dried tail may be seen there to this day, as a warning to any other smart, young lion that would be king.

THE FUNNEL MAKERS

The water buffaloes and the hogs used to come to a certain marsh during the heat of the day to wallow. Although there were more than enough mudholes for all, the buffaloes said the wallows, by right, belonged wholly to them. The hogs likewise claimed them.

One time Club Tail, the king of the buffaloes, said to Flat Nose, the king of the hogs:

"Flat Nose, you know very well that the buffaloes were the first wallowing animals; therefore all these mudholes are ours."

"You are mistaken," said Flat Nose, "the hogs were the first wallowers, so the mudholes are ours."

"Well," said old Club Tail, shaking his head, "if we buffaloes were not the first wallowers, you can't deny the fact that we are the biggest, and that ought to settle the matter. Be gone!"

So from that time on there was much quarreling between the different wallowers. The buffaloes tried to gore the hogs with their long horns, and the hogs tried to wound the buffaloes with their sharp tusks, but as the buffaloes were the larger they soon chased the hogs from the marsh.

Now Flat Nose was wonderfully wise so far as pig wisdom goes. One hot day the buffalo king found him and all his companions at the edge of the marsh, digging deep holes in the ground with their tough snouts.

"Pray, what are you doing?" asked Club Tail of Flat Nose.

"We are making funnels," said Flat Nose.

"Why are you making so many funnels?" asked Club Tail.

"Well," said Flat Nose, " since you will not let us use the wallows any more, we have decided to bore these holes through to the hollow of the earth, and drain the marsh. The water will soon run through; then your loose hide will become so dry that it will crack open, and your tongue will loll out at your mouth for lack of moisture. As for us, we have found a spring in a rocky place near the top of the mountain, and are going there as soon as we have drained the marsh. Please go away, as we have no time to talk."

When Club Tail heard what the hogs were going to do, he ran to the other buffaloes and told them about the matter.

"Come," said he, trembling all over, "let's make a treaty with the hogs before the water is all gone."

So the big, stupid animals ran to the hogs and begged them to make a treaty, on the condition that both the buffaloes and the hogs should share the wallows upon equal terms.

From then on the wallowers have gotten along in peace, and to this day one often sees a hog and a buffalo peacefully sharing the same mudhole.

MR. MONK AND THE QUARRELSOME ANIMALS

The deer and the gazelles had to leave the jungle and seek a new home, on account of the flesh eaters. They soon found an open country, with here and there a tamarind tree, and a long, clear lake near the center.

In this place they were safe from the lion, the tiger, and other large flesh eaters, for such animals do not like to venture into the open. They got along fairly well, but they did not like the frogs in the lake, nor the bees that hovered about the lotus flowers.

The frogs croaked all the time, and were never quiet, while the bees sometimes stung them on the legs when they waded into the water to get a drink. They were afraid to do anything to the bees, for the little creatures had a way of defending themselves against the largest enemy. They worried the poor, timid frogs by making them jump helter-skelter from their cool places on the rush-covered banks.

One day a flock of wild goats wandered into this open country.

"Friends," they said to the deer and gazelles, "we beg of you to let us live here in peace; in the jungle from which we fled the tigers are catching and eating our little ones every day."

"Do not call us friends," said an old deer, the king of the herds, "you are not of our kind; then, too, there is only enough grass here for ourselves. Be gone!" he exclaimed, stamping his foot.

"We are sorry," replied the goats, "we wanted to be neighborly, but since you do not care to be friendly, we shall have to get along as well as we can. Though you are unkind, we prefer your company to that of the tigers."

When the deer and the gazelles heard what the goats had to say they tried to chase them away, but the goats stayed in spite of them. From that time on the deer, the gazelles, and the goats quarreled and fought while the frogs sang in peace, and the bees sipped the nectar from the sweet-smelling lotus flowers.

One dark night a giant carried off the old king. Next morning there was great fear throughout the valley. For a time all the creatures stopped their quarreling.

"What are we to do? " they said. "We escaped from the tigers and the lions; now a worse enemy has found us." They tried to talk matters over peacefully, and plan some way to get rid of their common enemy, but it was not long until they began to quarrel again.

One night the animals lay down with aching bones, but were soon dreaming how they would resume the fight in the morning. About midnight they were awakened by the bleating of a gazelle as she was carried away by the terrible giant.

"Help me!" cried the poor gazelle, "please help me!" But they could do nothing in the dark. In the morning an old goat called the creatures together.

"I'm afraid we can do nothing ourselves," he said, "but perhaps the wise monkey could help us. Quick! Let's send a swift-footed deer to bring him."

So the deer ran as fast as he could to the jungle to get Mr. Monk. In a little while he returned with the wise monkey upon his back.

Mr. Monk hopped upon a stump, while all the animals gathered around him.

"Now," said he, "you fellows can easily get the better of these stupid giants if you'll only work together; but you can do nothing at all if you don't stop quarreling and fighting. Why, if you treat them kindly, even the frogs and the bees may be of help to you. Are you willing to make peace among yourselves? "

"We are! We are! We are!" shouted the deer, the gazelles, and the goats.

"Good! That is the way to talk," said the monkey. "Last night," he continued, "the giant passed under the tree where I live, carrying the gazelle, and I heard him say that he was coming back this evening with his brother to catch two more of you. Now when the two giants come do not be afraid, but as they take hold of their prey I want two of the hardest headed goats in the herd to back off and rush at them and butt them so hard that they'll not forget it as long as they live."

"We'll do the work," bleated two of the goats.

"That's the way to talk," said Mr. Monk. About sundown the two giants came lumbering into the valley. They seized a deer and a gazelle by the hind legs. To their great surprise the animals they caught did not appear frightened.

"Bless me!" exclaimed one of the giants, "what tame ones we've found!" Each of the giants then bent down in order to throw his prey over his shoulders.

"Go for them, boys!" shouted Mr. Monk.

No sooner had Mr. Monk said this than the goats butted the giants with their horns and hard heads and knocked them over, so that they let go of the animals they had caught.

"Oh!" groaned one of the giants a minute afterward, as he sat in the soft mud on the lake bank, "what a pain I have in my back and in my neck."

"Oh!" groaned the other, "it is not only my neck and back that pain me, but I ache all over. Come, brother, let us go. When we get well we'll bring ten of our friends here, but we'll have to hide in the water, so that we can rush upon the sleeping animals and carry them off before these horrible butting monsters know anything of our whereabouts."

They then got up and hobbled away, to the great amusement of the deer, the gazelles, and the goats, who were watching.

"That was a fine piece of work," said Mr. Monk to the goats, "but I am sorry that the two giants are coming back in a few days, with ten more of their kind. I think we can manage them all right, but I need a little time to think things over. I am pleased that you have made peace with one another, but I want you to do more. After this do not bother the frogs and the bees. You can move your sleeping ground so that the frogs' croaking will not disturb you. You can also change your drinking place to where there are no lotus flowers, so that you will not anger the bees. These little fellows may yet be of some help to you. Who can tell?"

"We'll do what you think best," replied the animals.

Every day Mr. Monk climbed to the top of a tall tree at the edge of the lake to look for the giants.

One afternoon, about a week later, he saw twelve big monsters making their way through the tall grass at the far end of the lake.

When they came to the edge of the lake, they waded into the water and soon disappeared below the surface, now and then poking up their noses to breathe. Before long he counted twelve long red noses, all in a row, sticking up out of the water not far from the edge of the lake nearest him.

He slid down the tree just in time to see several dozen frogs hop out of the water and blink in wonder at the twelve noses.

"You need not fear those fellows," said the monkey, "they are after bigger game. Do me a favor, and afterward you can sit upon the banks and croak to your heart's content."

"We will be glad to do what you ask," croaked the frogs. "What do you wish?"

"Hop back into the water and shake the lotus stems," said the monkey.

The frogs at once jumped into the water and began to shake the stems with all their might. The hundreds of bees that were on the flowers swarmed into the air.

Seeing the long noses sticking up out of the water they at once settled on them and began to drive in their sharp stingers.

Up went twenty-four big clumsy hands, which clawed at the twelve red noses. The bees covered the hands also, and both hands and noses sunk beneath the water, and up flew the bees.

In less than a minute, however, the twelve noses came up again. Down flew the bees, and down went the noses under the water again. The noses kept bobbing up and down until their owners were completely out of breath.

The giants then jumped up and ran bellowing down the

lake, waving their great arms like the fans of a windmill, and followed by a million bees. On they went until they came to a precipice, and as they could not see on account of their swollen eyes, they tumbled over the cliff, landing several hundred feet below.

Whether or not the giants were killed in the fall no one ever knew, but one thing is certain; they never came back to bother the animals again. After this the animals never troubled the frogs and the bees, but all lived together in peace.

THE TREMBLING TOWER

Tatlo was the son of a poor farmer. He lived in a little valley near the foot of a great mountain. As he was the oldest of a large family of children, he had to work hard in the rice fields to help his parents make a living.

At harvest time he would go into the fields with his sickle to cut the golden heads of rice. The rice was then tied into neat bundles and carried to high ground in the middle of the field. Here it was put into tall, narrow stacks to dry.

Later the bundles were spread around a pole set in a clean spot of ground, called the threshing yard. A great ox, with a brass ring in his nose, was then tied to the pole and driven round it to trample out the grain with his broad feet. The grain was afterwards winnowed, put into palm-leaf sacks, and stored in the house.

Tatlo's father sometimes raised more rice than he needed. Then he loaded the extra grain into a long boat, made by hollowing out a log, and floated it down the river to market.

One year when there was a large crop, Tatlo's father called his son, and said:

"Tatlo, you are now a young man; I want you to load the rice upon the boat and take it to the city."

The boy was very happy. It was the first time that such important work had been entrusted to him; then, too, it pleased him greatly to make a trip to the city, where he could see the stores, crowds of people, temples, and the ships from strange lands.

He worked all day, carrying the heavy bags of rice to the boat. Early the next morning he started floating down the river in the cool breeze. Near the bank of the river, a flock of pelicans was scooping up snails from the shallow water with their great bills, a tribe of monkeys chattered in the overhanging trees, and further away the parrots and hornbills were screaming and calling.

The fourth day after leaving home Tatlo came to still waters where he had to use the oars to propel the boat. When evening came, he was so tired that he decided to tie up and stay overnight.

Near the bank where he fastened the boat, stood a little house upon piles. In the house lived an old woman. When she saw Tatlo, she hobbled out with her cane to meet him.

"Where are you going, my lad?" she asked.

"I am going to the city to sell rice," replied Tatlo, "but I thought I would stay here until morning, as I am tired, and I would rather not land in the city at night."

"My home is yours," said the old woman, which meant that he was welcome to stay with her, "but I have nothing for you to eat but some roasted cashew nuts."

"Never mind," answered Tatlo, "I have plenty. Get me a dish and I shall give you some rice."

The old woman went into her house, and brought out an empty coconut shell. The boy filled the shell to the brim with rice, and then took from his food box a large fish that he had caught while coming down the river.

"La, la, la, la," sang the old woman when she saw the food. She threw down her cane, and began to spin round like a whirligig, to the great amusement of Tatlo. After a bit she hobbled to the house. Tatlo followed. He kindled a fire in the stove and helped to cook the meal.

When supper was over the old woman said:

"Tatlo, did you ever hear the story of the Fair Princess and the Trembling Tower?"

"No," he answered, "please tell the story to me."

"Well," began the old woman, "there was once a princess with a fair face whose father ruled over the White Tribe that lives beyond the great mountain. A wicked old ogre enchanted her. He then carried her away and fastened her with chains in the top of the high tower that stands upon the island in a lake near the city where you are going. Is this clear to you?" asked the old woman

"Yes, yes," replied Tatlo. "Go on with the story, and you shall have a bag of rice for your trouble."

"La, la, la, la," sang the old woman, "I never had as much as a bagful of rice in my life. This tower," she went on, "is guarded by forty fiery-headed monsters who live upon the small island. In the lake are forty huge crocodiles. Leading to the top of the tower is a ladder with a thousand steps. Every time anyone climbs up the ladder to try to rescue the princess, the monsters collect around the foot of the tower and begin to sing. The tower then trembles, trembles, trembles..." She stopped suddenly.

"Old woman, old woman, your story enchants me! "cried Tatlo. " Go on, go on! You shall have two bags of rice."

"La, la, la, la," sang the old woman again, "I never saw so much rice in all my life."

"As I was saying," she went on, "the tower trembles as if shaken by an earthquake. This tumbles the person on the ladder down to the lake where he is eaten by the crocodiles. But sometimes, so the story goes, a poor young man with a fair face and a kind heart will come along and rescue the princess." Again she stopped.

"Oh, finish the story, and you shall have three bags of rice," said Tatlo.

"La, la, la, la," sang the old woman, "I never even heard of so much rice in all my life."

"To rescue the princess," she said, "he must have two things: First, a magic ring that lies at the bottom of the river; and second, a coat of darkness that hangs in the ogre's castle at the top of the mountain. Anyone who wears the coat cannot be seen, and when he rubs the ring his enemies, if near him, will at once be turned into stone but the ring must not be used except in times of the greatest danger, when the coat is of no service. The name of this poor princess," the old woman went on, "is Pooty-pooty, and this in our language means 'pearly white.' Once a year the princess is allowed to come out upon the top of her tower. Only upon this day may she be seen, but the tower itself can be seen at any time, if the day is clear. They say she has been a prisoner in the tower for a hundred years, but she has never grown old, and is more beautiful now than when the wicked ogre stole her from her home."

"How can one get the coat and the ring?" asked Tatlo.

"I do not know," answered the old woman, "but I can tell you where the key that unlocks the tower is hidden. It is in a hole in the ladder near the fifth rung from the top."

"What day of the year can the princess be seen? " Tatlo asked eagerly.

"I forgot to tell you that," said the old woman. "Why, bless me! Tomorrow is the day. Tomorrow at sunrise I shall show her to you."

That night Tatlo could hardly sleep for thinking about the princess. He dreamed that he had found the ring and the coat, and had rescued her.

After breakfast the next morning the old woman took Tatlo to a spot a little distance from the house from which they could plainly see the tower. Just as the sun rose they saw the poor princess come out and look sadly toward the shore. Although the tower was several hundred feet high, they could see the beautiful princess very clearly.

When the two returned to the little house, Tatlo gave three bags of rice to the old woman, said goodbye to her, and hurried to his boat. As he pushed away from the bank, the old woman called:

"You have a fair face and a kind heart! Perhaps you are the young man that will rescue the princess. But do not try unless you can find the magic ring and the coat of darkness."

Tatlo did not stay long in the city. He did not enjoy seeing the stores and the crowds and the ships as he used to. He sold his rice, bought a few things, and started for home as soon as he could.

It took him nearly two weeks to row his boat back to his home, as traveling upstream was much harder than floating down stream and all the way he thought about the princess.

He could not forget the story, and it made him sad. One day his mother asked him why he was so unhappy. He then told her about the princess, and begged that he might be allowed to try to rescue her.

"Oh, son," said his mother when she heard the story, "it would be more than foolish for you to try. Remember that affairs of this kind are for princes, and not for peasants' sons."

Tatlo had made up his mind, however, to try to rescue the princess. He waited patiently until he was twenty-one years old, then he told his parents what he was going to do.

They were very sad to have him undertake such a hard task, but they at last agreed upon a day for his departure.

When the time came, Tatlo bade goodbye to his home, and, with a bundle under his arm, set out on foot for the city. He found the paths long and tiresome, but although footsore and weary he kept steadily on.

One day when he had come to the foot of a hill, he saw a fish flopping about in the grass on the bank of a large stream. He picked it up and carried it along with him, thinking he would cook it for his dinner.

On coming to a place where there was plenty of wood, he gathered up some dry sticks and built a fire. He was about to place the fish upon the hot flames when, to his great astonishment, it opened its mouth and said:

"Oh, please, please, put me back into the river."

Tatlo was very much surprised to hear a fish speak. The creature begged so earnestly for its life that Tatlo, hungry as he was, ran to the river and dropped it in the water. The fish at once dived beneath the surface, making a great splash as it went. In a moment it appeared again, and said:

"Thank you, young man of the fair face, for saving my life. What can I do to show my gratitude? What do you ask, O young man of the fair face?"

"Bring me the ring, the magic ring, at the bottom of the river," commanded Tatlo, quick as a flash.

The fish at once dived to the bottom of the river and brought up the ring. Much pleased, Tatlo placed the ring upon his finger, and the fish disappeared.

Overjoyed at his good fortune, Tatlo forgot his hunger and again set out upon his journey. During the afternoon he came to a great crag that jutted out from the side of the mountain. In a hole near the foot of the crag, Tatlo saw a young bird sitting in a nest. As he was very hungry, he thought he would cook it for his supper. When he reached out to seize it, the bird stretched out its neck, opened its wide mouth, and seemed to cry:

"Oh, I am hungry! I am hungry! Please give me something to eat."

Tatlo at once took what little food he had, dropped some into the young bird's mouth, and placed some more close beside the nest, and went on his way.

The next day Tatlo was so weak from lack of food that he could scarcely walk. He lay down by the side of the road to rest.

As he looked up into the sky he noticed a dark spot. Nearer and nearer the object came, until he saw that it was a great bird flying directly toward him. He tried to run, but he was too weak to do so. He fully expected to be carried away in the huge bird's talons.

The bird, however, circled about over the tree tops, then settled upon the ground near him, and said:

"You saved my nestling, O young man of the fair face. Two favors this day shall I grant you. Command what you will, and I shall obey you."

"First," said Tatlo, "bring me something to eat." Immediately the great bird flew away, and soon returned with a large piece of meat.

"Thank you," said Tatlo. "While I am cooking the meat, please fly to the ogre's castle at the top of yonder high mountain and bring me the coat of darkness."

"That is a very hard thing to do," replied the bird. "The ogre keeps the coat locked in a dungeon beneath the castle, but I shall get it for you, if I can."

She then flew off toward the distant mountain. For a week Tatlo watched the castle, hoping to catch sight of the friendly bird. He had about given up, when one evening he saw a dark speck moving among the clouds.

It grew larger and larger and to his great joy he saw that it was the bird with the coat in her beak. The bird did not alight, but when directly over the boy's head she dropped the coat, and turning, flew swiftly away to her nest.

Putting the precious garment under his arm, Tatlo continued his journey. When he reached the city he hired a small sailboat to take him to the island where the tower stood. As he left the wharf, a crowd of people who had heard that he was going to try to rescue the princess called to him to give up the attempt.

"Many have gone upon this foolish errand," they said, "but no one has ever come back."

In spite of all that was said, Tatlo unfurled the sails and sped away in the direction of the island.

On reaching the shore, he tied the boat to a tree at the edge of the water, put on his coat of darkness, and quietly walked to the tower. At the foot he saw the forty fiery-headed monsters standing silent and watchful, and the forty crocodiles asleep and motionless upon the rocks in the lake.

Though he knew the monsters could not see him with his coat of darkness on, Tatlo was very careful to make no sound. He stepped with greatest care upon the lowest rung of the ladder and began to climb. Up, up, he went, but the tower was so high that he thought he would never reach the top.

Tatlo was overjoyed to see the bird with the coat in her beak.

Finally he grew so tired and hot that he took off his coat and sat down upon one of the steps to rest. Suddenly he heard a great noise below, for the monsters had seen him as soon as he had taken off his coat.

At once the tower began to tremble as if shaken by a terrible earthquake, while the monsters formed in a circle around the foot of it and began to sing:

"Tremble, tremble, tower, tremble,
Waters roll and beasts assemble,
Round and round the foot we go
Dancing in a circle, ho
As we do it
He will rue it.
Tumble, tumble, Tatlo, tumble."

The great tower shook as it had never shaken before. Poor Tatlo held fast to the coat and clung to the ladder with all his might, but at length the coat was shaken out of his hand and fell to the ground.

As he swung dizzily back and forth like a pendulum he remembered the ring. Quick as thought he rubbed it against his sleeve. No sooner had he done so than the monsters stopped singing, and the tower became still.

Tatlo drew a great breath of relief. He rested a few minutes and then began to climb the ladder again. At last he reached the fifth rung and there was the key just as the old woman had told him it would be.

On he went to the top of the tower, and unlocked the door. He found the princess, who was rejoiced to see him. Tatlo quickly undid the chains on her ankles, took her in his arms, and carried her safely down the ladder. He found the monsters turned to stone standing in a circle around the foot of the tower, but no longer to be feared. The crocodiles also seemed turned to stone, for they made no move as he approached.

The happy young people had little trouble in finding their way to the White Tribe. The people received them joyfully, and a few months later crowned Tatlo and Pootypooty their king and queen. Thereafter they lived happily in a palace, and ruled their subjects wisely.

One time—so the story goes—as King Tatlo was engaged with his advisors over an important matter of state, he heard a famiiiar voice in the courtyard below.

"La, la, la, la," sang the voice, "my three bagfuls of rice gave out, but I know the king will give me some more. La, la, la, la. It's three long months that I've been on the journey. La, la, what a fine palace this is!"

The king hurried down to the courtyard. "Old woman, old woman," he said, "you shall live in my palace and have all the rice you can eat as long as you live."

"La, la, la, la," sang the old woman again, as she spun round and round like a whirligig, to the great amusement of Tatlo Junior and the rest of the bystanders.

MR. MONK AND THE FRIGHTENED ANIMALS

Old Jojo was a mighty hunter who lived in a little house in the middle of a great forest. He had a dog, a horse, a cat, and a rooster. He had other pets, but these were the ones he liked best. The dog he called Ayso, the horse Byso, the cat Pooso, and the rooster Maynook.

When Jojo died, his favorite pets lay down, one by one, and grieved themselves to death. The neighbors buried them all together in one large grave not far from the house. Around the grave they built a stone wall, on one side of which they placed a marble slab with this inscription:

Here Lies Jojo,
The Mighty Hunter.
With Him Are Buried Ayso,
His Dog, Byso,
His Horse, Pooso,
His Cat,
And

Maynook, His Rooster.
May They Rest
In Peace.

The forest people were all very happy when they learned that Jojo and his pets were gone. The forest now became such a peaceful place that the wild hogs slept under the old hunter's house, the deer ate the vines in his garden, and the buffaloes rubbed their sides against the stone wall of the grave.

But this peace did not last long. Jojo had been dead scarcely a year when some of the more timid creatures said they heard strange noises about the old house, such as the grinding of corn, the whetting of spears, and the mending of nets. The story that Jojo had come to life soon spread among the forest people.

A month or two later Tusker, the wild boar, came running as fast as he could to the tree in which the wise monkey lived. Gnashing his teeth, and with his bristles standing upon end, he exclaimed: "Oh, Mr. Monk, Jojo has come to life again. I have heard his voice three times, but I cannot see him, neither can I smell him. Today, about noon, the voice woke me from my lair. I ran to the top of the mountain where I stopped to get my breath, but I had scarcely stopped when I heard the voice a second time. I then ran to the other side of the mountain, where I lay down for a rest but scarcely had I closed my eyes when I heard the voice again. What shall I do? I can hear the twang of bowstrings and the hissing of spears now."

"Tusker," said the monkey, "you are silly indeed to think that you heard the voice of Jojo, the hunter. I really believe that what you heard was the ticks in your ears. Lie down in that clump of bushes over there, and go to sleep. I will keep a close watch from the forks of this tree, and if I should see a man I will let you know in time to get away."

The boar hid himself in the bushes and went to sleep.

Next morning Crinkle Horn, the wild buffalo, came running as fast as he could to see the monkey. Pawing the ground and rubbing his horns upon a rock, he began to bellow:

"Oh, Mr. Monk, Jojo's horse has come to life again. Before it was dawn I heard him neighing in the valley, as if answering the call of his master. What shall I do? I feel one of Jojo's snares tightening about my neck every time I run through a dark place, and I really believe there are a half a dozen of his arrows sticking in my back this minute."

"Quiet your nerves, Crinkle Horn," said the monkey. "What you heard was a harmless owl; what you ran into was a tangled vine; and the arrows you feel in your back are but the bites of the cowflies. Bless me, if I do not see a half a dozen big ones driving their bills into your tough hide now. Brush them off with your long tail, then go out there and stay with Tusker."

The buffalo hid in the bushes with the boar.

Later Fleetfoot, the deer, came running as fast as he could to the home of the monkey. Scared half to death, he exclaimed:

"Oh, Mr. Monk, Jojo's dog has come to life again. Last night I heard him barking in the forest, but I can neither see him nor smell him. What shall I do? I can see Jojo's nets stretched across all the dark places, and hear the footsteps of his hound close at my heels, crushing the leaves."

"You have more horns than brains, Fleetfoot," replied the monkey. "What you thought was a dog's bark was perhaps the croak of a frog, the deer nets were but strong cobwebs, and the footsteps at your heels were no doubt but the dragging of a weed caught in the hairs of your tail. Bless me, if I don't see the weed hanging there now! Shake it off, then go out there and stay with Tusker and Crinkle Horn."

The deer hid himself in the bushes with the boar and the buffalo. The monkey stretched himself out on the shady side of a limb for a nap. He had slept but a few moments when he heard a squeaky voice close to his ear. Opening his eyes, he saw Slick Tail, the rat.

"Oh, Mr. Monk," squeaked the rat, "Jojo's cat has come to life, again. Last night as I lay sleeping with my family, I was awakened by Pooso's mewing. When I peeped out of my den in the hollow log, I saw his eyes shining like two moons. What shall I do? I feel his sharp claws in my sides now."

"Slick Tail," replied the monkey, "what you heard was perhaps the call of some harmless nightbird; what you saw was a couple of lightning bugs; and what you feel is a thorn in your sides. Bless me, if I don't see the thorn now. Pull it out with your teeth, then go out there and stay with Tusker, Crinkle Horn, and Fleetfoot."

The rat hid himself in the bushes with the boar, the buffalo, and the deer.

Next morning as the monkey climbed down the tree in search

"Pull the thorn out with your teeth, Slick Tail," said the monkey.

of his breakfast, Sawshanks, a big locust, flew in a circle about him and chirped excitedly:

"O Mr. Monk, Jojo's rooster has come to life again. What shall I do? I just now heard his crowing in the mango tree near his master's house. I can feel his strong bill pinching me in two."

"Quiet yourself, Sawshanks," said the monkey. "What you heard was perhaps the cry of a gecko, and what you feel is the pressing of your legs against your body. Fly out there to those bushes and stay with Tusker, Crinkle Horn, Fleetfoot, and Slick Tail."

The locust hid himself in the bushes with the boar, the buffalo, the deer, and the rat.

The monkey breakfasted upon some ripe bananas, which he found growing on a tree in Jojo's yard. He then looked carefully about the place, but he could neither see nor smell any sign of man, beast, or fowl. While going back to his home, he passed the bushes in which the boar, the buffalo, the deer, the rat, and the locust were hid.

"Friends," he said as he came near them, "I have just come from Jojo's house, and I could not see, hear, nor smell anything, which would show that Jojo or any of his pets had come to life. When the sun goes down, I want you to go over there together and watch. If you see or hear anything strange about the place, come back and tell me.'

When the sun went down the boar, the buffalo, the deer, the rat, and the locust went to Jojo's place. Everything about the house was very quiet; but suddenly there came such terrible sounds, that the creatures rushed pell-mell into the jungle.

In the morning they all came to report to the monkey. "Oh," chirped the locust, "last night as we passed the stone wall, I heard Jojo's rooster crow."

"Oh," squeaked the rat, "last night as we passed the stone wall I heard Jojo's cat mew."

"Oh," said the deer, "last night as we passed the stone wall, I heard Jojo's dog bark."

"Oh," said the buffalo, "last night as we passed the stone wall, I heard Jojo's horse neigh."

"Oh," said the boar, "last night as we passed the stone wall, I heard the voice of Jojo."

"Yes, yes," they all cried together, "we heard the rooster crow, the cat mew, the dog bark, the horse neigh, and Jojo shout. They've all come back again! They've all come back again!"

"Well," said the monkey as he scratched his head, "there is something strange about this. Go out to the bushes and hide yourselves again and I shall search further."

The boar, the buffalo, the deer, the rat, and the locust hid themselves in the thicket, while the monkey set out a second time to visit Jojo's place.

In the house he found some old nets, traps, snares, bows, spears, and other things that Jojo had used. In one corner was a large, wooden bucket filled with tar. Nothing was there to show that any living thing had been in the house for a long time. The monkey then walked out to the stone wall. He looked over it, but there, also, he saw no signs of any living thing. As he sat down to think matters over along came Sharpnose, the mongoose.

"Good morning, Mr. Monk," said the mongoose. "Good morning, Sharpnose," said the monkey.

"How goes everything?" asked the mongoose.

"Very well," replied the monkey, "only that my sleep has been disturbed lately by different creatures of the forest, who run to me at all times of the day and night, saying that they have either heard the voice of Jojo, or else the voices of his pets. They have got it into their heads that Jojo and all his family have come back alive. I came here to look about a bit, but I fail to find any sign of life at all."

"Rather strange," replied the mongoose. "Perhaps I can be of some help to you."

"You surely can," replied the monkey. "You have a much keener nose than I. Please sniff around the place and tell me if you smell anything unusual."

The mongoose climbed upon the wall. Putting his nose close to the surface of a flat stone he drew in a deep breath.

"Do you smell anything? " asked the monkey.

"I do," replied the mongoose, a little puzzled.

"Pray, what is it? "

"I do not know."

"Is it a man?"

"No."

"A horse?"

"No."

"A cat?"

"No."

"A rooster?"

"No—but that makes me think," replied the mongoose. "While it is not a rooster that I smell, I am sure it is some kind of bird."

"Is it a crow?" asked the monkey.

"No."

"An eagle? "

"No."

"A duck?"

"No—but that makes me think," replied Sharpnose. "The bird I smell looks like a duck in one way; he has a large bill, but his bill—"

The monkey did not give the mongoose time to finish, but laughed:

"Oh, no, no! He's neither chicken, crow, eagle, nor duck. He's a parrot, old Jojo's parrot! They tell me he's a hundred years old. What a pity it is that they did not bury the creature with the rest!"

The monkey ran back to the thicket.

"Well, friends," he cried, "if you want to see me catch the thing that's been making all this trouble, come with me tonight."

A little before dark the buffalo, the boar, the deer, the rat, and the locust hid themselves behind a stone. The monkey concealed himself in the grass at the bottom of the wall. Near him he had placed the bucket of tar.

Soon the parrot flew down from a tall tree to the wall, and uttered a loud crow. He had just begun to squall like an old tomcat, when the monkey seized him by the legs.

"Squawk, squawk!" the parrot cried, as he tried to get free.

"Never mind your squawking," said the monkey and he dipped the parrot into the tar.

"It seems that I have not only caught the rooster, but the cat, the dog, the horse, and Jojo, all in one."

When morning came, the jungle people for miles around came to see the parrot with the black tarry coat.

Before the tar finally wore off, the old bird flew to the other side of the mountain, and has never been seen since. And the forest became a place of peace once more.

THE GIANT LAMPONG

Lampong was a giant. He was terribly ugly, and of great size and strength. Yet he was a harmless fellow, at first at any rate.

He lived all alone in a cave at the head of a gorge, on the side of a mountain. During the threshing season the farmers would hire him to stamp out the grain, because his broad, flat feet, each of which was fully a yard long, were better for that purpose than those of a dozen oxen.

They would also put a heavy harness upon him and hitch him to the long sweep of the cane mill at sugar-making time. Round and round he would go with three or four children on his back, while the great wooden rollers of the mill crushed the juice from the stalks.

As might have been expected from his size, the giant was a huge eater, but he was concerned about the quantity of food, and not the quality. Two cooks were employed by the farmers to prepare his meals, which usually consisted of a cartload of pumpkins mixed with rice, ears of corn, onions, and chickens, all of which was boiled in a great iron kettle. When this were done, the cooks would turn it out into a large wooden trough to cool.

When dinner time came the giant would sit at the side of his trough, and shovel the food into his huge mouth, using a ladle that would hold a bucketful.

Sometimes Lampong would sit cross-legged upon the ground and open his cavelike mouth, while children amused themselves by tossing watermelons and coconuts into it. He ate the melons, rinds and all, but only the meat of the coconuts, letting the pieces of cracked shells work out at the corners of his lips.

Lampong would never take money for his work, because he did not know the value of it. Instead he always received his wages in toll. At the end of the week he would hold open a great bag made from an oxhide. Into this the farmers would pour his share of the grain or sugar, as the case might be.

Sometimes, when he was well supplied with these articles, he would take as his pay several dozen chickens, or perhaps a pig. He would then throw his bag over his shoulder and go home.

One year when the rice and sugar crops were better than usual, Lampong grew fat and lazy from eating so much, and the farmers could not get him to work for them.

He had a large supply of food stored in his cave, and like an old fat bear in winter time he stayed in his cave and slept.

When his food gave out, he crawled forth and walked down the gorge in the direction of the farm lands. At the edge of the valley he met a farmer, going home from the fields.

"Hello, Lampong!" said the farmer, "are you looking for work?"

"No," replied the giant. "I am tired of being somebody's ox. Hereafter I shall get my living in an easier way." So saying, he strode on toward a corn field.

Next morning a farmer discovered that a thief had been in his corn, and had carried off a half a wagon load of roasting ears. Tracks and other signs plainly showed that Lampong was the guilty one.

In the middle of the field there was a sandy spot. In this the giant had wallowed, for he had a custom of rolling in the soft dirt, much the same as a horse does.

The farmers did not wish to shoot the big fellow, for they hoped they could break him of the bad habit of stealing so that he would work for them again. The farmer who owned the cornfield said:

"Let's gather up all the burrs and thorns we can find and scatter them in Lampong's wallow. Perhaps that will cure him."

"That's a fine idea," said the other farmers.

So they gathered burrs, thorns, and other pricking things After they had collected a great quantity, they spread them thickly over the sandy place.

That night when Lampong had filled his oxhide bag full of roasting ears, he lay down for a comfortable roll in the sand.

He had given but a few turns when his hair was filled with burrs, and his skin bristled with thorns. He jumped up, bellowing, but as it was quite dark he could not see what was causing the trouble.

Thinking that some kind of biting insects had got into his wallowing place, he ran to a hard spot not far away, where he lay down and rolled about in an effort to dislodge them. This only sent the burrs deeper into his tangle of hair and drove the thorns deeper into his tough skin. So he got up, took to his heels, and did not stop running until he reached his cave.

It took Lampong the greater part of a week to pick all the burrs out of his hair, and to pull all the thorns from his skin. When he set forth upon another thieving expedition he did not go to the corn field, you may be sure.

This time he went to the fish traps at the wide mouth of the river where it emptied into the sea. Wading out into the water with his bag over his shoulder, he reached into the traps with his long arms and drew out all the fish, which he dropped into his bag.

He started home, but had not gone far when he met a crab fisher, with a sack of crabs hung on his back. Seeing Lampong with his booty, the crab fisher called out:

"I see that you are up to your tricks again. Why don't you go to work like an honest fellow?"

"I'm nobody's ox!" roared the ugly giant, as he threw down his bag and started for the crab fisher.

He soon caught the man, and tossed him up into the air as high as the tree tops. Lampong then dropped upon his back, and with his upturned feet caught the fisherman as he came down.

With his broad feet he turned him round and round as a juggler does a ball, roaring with laughter all the time. This shook the string loose from the mouth of the crab bag, that still hung on the fisherman's back.

The crabs at once fell upon Lampong, and as they were angry from their shaking they took hold of him in a hundred places with their strong, sharp pincers.

The giant's fun was thus very suddenly turned into a painful experience. He threw the fisherman to the ground, jumped to his feet, and ran bellowing to his cave, the crabs hanging on to him and nipping him without mercy.

The crabs took hold of Lampong in a hundred places.

Lampong did not return to the fish traps, neither did he go into the corn fields again.

In about a month, however, the farmers discovered that something had happened to their coconut groves. They found that Lampong had been shaking the trees so hard that not only the ripe nuts had fallen off, but the green ones as well.

The farmers now began to talk of banding together to catch the giant, and to put him in jail at night and make him work by day. There were several things, however, that stood in the way of this plan.

In the first place, they were afraid if they tried to force him to work in harness he would become angry, and not only tear up the harness, but the mill, plow, or whatever else he was hitched to. Should they force him to break rocks, it would be necessary to employ half a dozen carpenters to make handles for the sledge hammers, for he would break them as fast as they could be put in. Then there was the problem of feeding him, and last but not least, the townspeople objected to having him in jail at night, because he snored so loud that no one could sleep within a quarter of a mile of him.

At last they decided to try to scare him out of the country. In the coconut grove, where he had been coming at night, they placed several large earthenware jars filled with strong palm wine.

That night the big fellow drank every drop of the wine and toward morning crawled to his cave, overcome by it.

The next day, in the middle of the morning, a number of men with crowbars and axes placed themselves along the edge of the gorge that led to the cave.

Two men went to the cave, where they found the giant lying upon his back, sound asleep, and snoring so loud that it made the hills roar.

One of the men stood above the opening of the cave, while the other took a long pole and pushed off a lot of earth above Lampong's head.

Lampong scrambled to his feet and ran from the cave, but as he poked his head out the man above the door rolled down a big rock. The giant in alarm tore down the gorge as fast as he could.

He had not gone far when some men above pried loose an overhanging rock, as big as a house. Down it came with a mighty crash, smashing trees and everything else in its path. It landed at the bottom of the gorge in front of the fleeing giant.

He climbed over it, then ran faster than ever, dodging stones as they came tumbling from the banks high above him. At the deepest part of the gorge several big trees fell into his path, and he had great trouble getting through the tangled mass of branches and trunks.

When Lampong reached the seashore, he found many people running to and fro as if in great excitement.

"What is the matter?" he asked, almost out of breath.

"Oh, Lampong," they shouted, "run for your life; the mountains are falling down; the mountains are falling down!"

Farther along the beach he met other people.

"Run, Lampong, run! " they screamed, "the mountains are falling down!" and he ran still faster.

Soon he came upon a great crowd of men, women, and children, wringing their hands and crying. As Lampong passed, they asked:

"What is the matter, Lampong? Please tell us what is happening."

"Blockheads!" bellowed the giant, "did you not know that the mountains were falling down?"

"No, no," they replied, "but if that is the case we shall jump into yonder boat and sail away to where there are no mountains. Come," they called to one another, "let's get into the boat before the mountains tumble upon our heads!"

Upon hearing this, Lampong jumped into the boat. He quickly untied it, and away he went in the direction of Indo-China.

As the sails were already set, with a wind blowing full into them, the boat sped away, and was soon out of sight. Several years later—so the story goes—a sailor came home and reported that he had seen Lampong in faraway Bangkok at work, side by side with one of the king's elephants, dragging a teakwood log down the street toward the royal palace. That may be true. Anyway Lampong was never seen again in his native land.

THE BEES AND THE KATYDIDS

When the world was still young, the bees and the katydids met on the same day, but at different places, to talk over matters concerning the public welfare.

The bees assembled on the outside of a big, hollow tree, and at once chose a speaker.

"Let us elect a ruler," said the speaker.

"Good," buzzed all the bees together.

So they elected a queen.

"Now," continued the spokesman, "let's appoint certain of our members to gather honey, others wax, others beebread, others to look after the queen and the young, but when it comes to fighting let us all fight together."

"Fine," buzzed all the bees together.

So the bees moved into the hollow tree, and forthwith began to put into practice all the things that they had agreed upon.

With the katydids, things turned out differently. As each wore a crown, each insisted upon being the king; as each was bedecked in a priestly robe, each wanted to be high priest. Also each wanted to be a general, because each carried a shield, and each wanted to lead the band, because each had his own music box. The place of workman no one wanted, although each one carried two saws.

After wrangling a long time, the meeting of the katydids ended with a grand chorus, in a last effort to bring about a better feeling. In this they also made a mess of things, because each one insisted upon being the director, and sang in his own way. One made a noise like a distant tapping of an anvil, another like the melancholy chirrup of a cricket, still another like the clatter of a snaredrum. The result was a miserable discord, and the meeting broke up in a general fight. After the scramble, the katydids all flew back to the trees, leaving matters in a worse state than before.

Said an old fellow, who had been the cause of a lot of the trouble:

"I'll be my own king, priest, soldier, musician—and workman." When he had ended this speech, which was heard by no one but himself, he at once set up a hoarse tune upon his music box. A sleeping bird in the branches of the tree above was awakened by the terrible noise, and flew down and gobbled him up. So that was the end of king, priest, soldier, musician, and workman.

Today, wherever you find the bees you will see that they get along peaceably and happy. The katydids, however, live for themselves, and whenever a few of them get together, they bite and fight each other like savages. When winter comes the bees live in a warm home and feast upon bread and honey, while most of the quarrelsome katydids either freeze to death or starve.

THE WISE MORO AND THE HINDU RIDDLE GUESSER

Many years ago, there was a Hindu who claimed that he could guess the most difficult riddle. He had been in all parts of the world, and no one had ever been able to give him a riddle that he could not guess. One time he went to the fair at Manila where he set up a booth, and sent out a crier to tell the people that he was ready for business. For each riddle he guessed, he charged a *peseta,* and for each one he failed to guess, he promised a large bag of gold. But no one had ever been able to make a riddle that he could not guess.

A great crowd of people surrounded the Hindu, and when they saw the bag of gold they were anxious to try their luck. But as fast as the riddles were propounded the Hindu guessed them, and in a few hours he had filled a small trunk with money. Those who lost their money went away grumbling, but as fast as they went away others came to take their places.

At length a wise Moro from Sulu came up to the Hindu's booth, and said, "Mr. Fakir, I can make a riddle that you cannot guess in five minutes, or in five years."

"Sir," said the Hindu, somewhat ruffled at the bantering spirit of the Moro, "if you will make a riddle that I cannot guess in five minutes I will not only give you the bag of gold, but I will throw in this trunkful of money for good measure. Come on with your riddles; let them be one, or one hundred."

The Moro's first riddle:

When the lake dries
The heron dies.

"That," said the Hindu, without batting an eye, "is a lamp. The blaze is the heron, and the oil in the bowl is the lake. Next!"

And the Hindu raked the Moro's money into his box.

The Moro's second riddle:

When I see its face it is my uncle,
but when I see its back it is my aunt.

"A Chinaman!" came the answer, but not so quick as the first. "A Chinaman has a man's face, but his long braid of hair makes the back of his head look like a woman's."

And the Hindu raked the Moro's money into his box.

The Moro's third riddle:

Daniel was put in prison, but he did not suffer.
Instead, it was the prison that suffered.

"A little harder than the others," said the Hindu, "but still I would call it a child's riddle. *Daniel,* was a thorn in the flesh. The thorn did not suffer, but the flesh, which was the prison, did. Come on with something that will make me think!"

And the Hindu raked the Moro's money into his box.

The Moro's fourth riddle:

There was a boat full of passengers, all of the same color.
At the end of a three weeks' voyage there were among
the passengers white people, yellow people, brown people,
red people, and black people; also people of mixed colors.
Yet the boat never took on any new passengers.

The Hindu had to think a little over this one, but at the end of a couple of minutes he said: "The boat was a hen's nest filled with eggs from different breeds of chickens. The eggs, which were of the same color, were the passengers; and when the chicks hatched they were of many colors."

And the Hindu raked the Moro's money into his box.

The Moro's fifth riddle:

He wears a crown, but is not a king;
he dresses in a priestly robe, but is not a priest;
he carries a shield, but is not a soldier,'
he carries a fiddle, but is only a noise maker;
he has two saws, but is not a carpenter;
he chews tobacco, but is not a Spaniard.

The Hindu thought deeply for three minutes, and then said: "That is a crested grasshopper; I do not think any explanations are necessary. Come on with another, or else step aside and let someone else give me a riddle."

And the Hindu raked the Moro's money into his box.

The Moro's sixth riddle:

The mountain is wearing down;
the ant hill is bearing flowers;
the candles are growing dim;
and the two are now three.

When the riddle guesser heard this, he shut his eyes and fell back as if asleep, but just before the five minutes were up he opened them, and shouted, "An old man!" Taking a long breath he explained the riddle in this manner: "The man's body is the mountain, his head is the ant hill, his white hair the flowers, the dim candles are his eyes, and the staff he walks with makes his two legs three."

And the Hindu raked the Moro's money into his box.

The Moro's seventh riddle:

Two bony-backed twin brothers, each with four lean hounds—the hounds all being of the same litter—went boar-hunting upon a mountain covered with a thick forest. When the hunters had reached a place near the top of the mountain they found where the boars had been rooting in the ground, and it was not long until the dogs bayed the animals. "Alas!" said one of the hunters to his brother, "we brought neither bows nor spears. How shall we kill the game?" "Stupid one," replied the other brother, "what's to hinder us from slaying the boars by pressing them between our hard backs?" And they proceeded to slay them in that manner.

When the Hindu heard the seventh riddle, he began to scratch his head. First he scratched it with his right hand, then with his left, then with both hands. He scratched and he scratched, but he could not think of an answer. At last he had to give it up.

And the Moro carried off the Hindu's bag of gold and trunkful of money.

Here is the answer the Hindu could not guess:

The bony-backed brothers are the thumbs; the eight hounds are the fingers, the mountain is the head, and the hair is the forest.

MR. MONK AND THE TIGER

A big old tiger used to come down out of the mountain at night to steal the pigs, calves, and sheep of the farmers who lived in the valleys.

One time a farmer made a strong trap by setting poles in the ground like a stockade. Over the top he placed other poles, tying them down with strips of rattan. He made a heavy door of thick boards and fastened it in such a manner, with a string tied to a trigger, that when an animal passed within he would step upon the trigger. This would release the door, which would at once fall down and make him a prisoner.

When the farmer had finished the trap, he baited it with a piece of meat. That night the old tiger went forth from his home in the jungle to steal an animal for his supper. He had not gone far when he began to sniff the air.

"Meat," he said to himself. "Some farmer has killed a pig today and hung him up somewhere. I'll just follow my nose until it leads me to the meat; then I'll have a good supper without having the trouble of catching a pig. Their squealing upsets me sometimes. I like to find them already killed and dressed."

Soon the tiger came to the trap. "Ah, what a nice little house that farmer has made to keep his pork in!" said the tiger. "And he's gone off and forgotten to shut the door."

In walked the tiger, stepping right on the trigger, but he was so intent upon getting the meat that he did not hear the door as it closed from behind.

When he had eaten the pork he turned around to walk out, but to his great surprise he found himself a prisoner. He scratched the door with his long, sharp claws, threw himself against the walls, and even jumped so high that he hit his head against the roof, in an effort to get free. After a while he lay down, beat the floor with his tail, and roared.

An old hog not far away heard the roaring, and not knowing what it was, came up to the trap, where he found the tiger crying in a very pitiful manner.

"Oh, Granddad," cried the tiger, "please put the end of your strong nose under that door and lift it up so that I can get out of this trap."

"They tell me that tigers are fond of pork," said the hog, "and I am afraid you would eat me up if I turned you loose."

"I will have to admit that I have eaten a few hogs," cried the tiger, "but I am not nearly so guilty as many other tigers that I know; I have an uncle that has eaten more than a hundred hogs. Just let me out, please, and I promise you on the word of an honest tiger, that I will never taste hogflesh again, though I should live a thousand years."

"I cannot trust you," grunted the hog, and he walked off.

"Please do not leave me," pleaded the tiger. "Let me out and I shall tell all the tigers in the country how kind you were to me. Then you will never have to fear a tiger again."

"No," answered the hog.

Just then an owl hooted in a tree near-by. "What was that?" asked the hog.

"That was the soft purr of my uncle," said the tiger, "but do not be afraid; just let me out of this trap and I shall tell him not to eat you."

The hog came back to the trap. The owl uttered a loud scream.

"Hurry!" said the tiger; "my uncle gets your scent. Let me out before it is too late."

The silly old hog placed the tough end of his nose under the door and lifted it.

Out slipped the tiger. He stretched himself, licked his chops, then pounced upon the hog and ate him.

The ungrateful tiger went back to the mountains, where he lay down and went to sleep. He had eaten so much that he was not hungry again for a week. When he went forth again to find another meal he came upon the trap a second time. This time the trap was baited with a real live pig, tied to a stake driven into the ground at the end opposite the door.

"Oh!" said the tiger aloud, when he saw the pig, "if I only knew how to get out of that trap after I got in, I would have that nice fat pig; I am so hungry."

"Hello, Ringtail," shouted a monkey from the top of a tree. "What were you saying?"

"I said," replied the tiger, "that I wished I knew how to go into this thing, without being made a prisoner."

"That's easy when one knows how," said the monkey as he slid down the tree. "I can walk in and out of a trap whenever I wish."

"Let me see you do it," said the tiger.

The monkey walked into the trap, but he was very careful not to touch the trigger. He then walked out, to the great astonishment of the tiger.

"Will you teach me how to do that? " asked the tiger.

"Yes," replied the monkey, "but you must agree to two things: first, that you'll let me untie this poor innocent little pig, so that he may go home in peace; second, that you will never come back to these parts again. I am tired of hearing you roar at night. I've hardly slept since you were here the other time."

"Of course, you may turn the pig loose," said the tiger. "As to my roaring, I'll not only stop roaring myself when near your home, but I'll tell my uncle, whose voice is ten times louder than mine, never to open his mouth while within twenty miles of this place. Not only that, my dear uncle and I shall seek feeding grounds at the farthest edge of the forest. I am an honest tiger, Mr. Monk, and you can always depend upon what I say. Ask anyone, who knows me, if you are not willing to take my word."

The monkey had to laugh at the idea of an honest tiger. "All honest tigers," he said to himself, "are dead tigers."

The monkey then ran in and out of the trap several times, taking care each time not to touch the trigger.

"Well, honest fellow, did you see how I did it?" he asked the tiger after several trips.

"I am quite sure that I understand now," answered the tiger.

The monkey walked back to the end of the trap and began to untie the pig. While he was doing this, the tiger poked his head in at the door. When the pig saw the tiger's cruel eyes staring at him, he was terribly frightened, and drew back.

"Let me see you walk into the trap," said the tiger.

"Why does the pig not come out?" asked the tiger.

"He's afraid you will not keep your word," said the monkey. "Run away into the woods a couple of miles and roar to show the frightened pig that it is safe for him to go home. You can then come back and I shall show you more about the trap."

"I know all about the trap now," said the old tiger as he poked his head farther in.

"Look out, or you will be caught!" shouted the monkey.

"Oh, no, I won't, Mr. Monk," said the tiger. "You do not think I am silly enough to put my foot on that little piece of wood again, do you?"

The monkey walked out past the tiger that was slipping inch by inch into the trap. He stood near the opening and waited until the tiger was in all but his tail. He then jerked the string that was fastened to the trigger. Bang! Crashed the door down on the tiger's tail, close up to his body.

When the pig heard the crash he squeezed his little body through the bars, and did not stop running until he was safe at home with his mother.

"Wow, w-o-o-w! " roared the tiger. His frightful roaring woke all the farmers in the country, who came running to the scene with all the weapons they could lay their hands upon.

"Oh, ho! " exclaimed the man who had set the trap, "we have him safe this time, and bless me, if the pig didn't get away!"

The next time you see a tiger-skin rug, it may be the one that was made from the hide of the wicked old flesh-eating tiger that you have been reading about in this story.

BRISTLEPATE AND THE SAD PRINCESS

There was once a young lad who was called Bristlepate. The children called him so because his stiff, bristly hair stuck out in every direction. Bristlepate was different from the other boys and girls who lived round about. He was not content to cut wood as they were. He loved his flute, and was always ready to play at a wedding, a dance, or any kind of party. His parents were makers of clay pots. They always needed wood for their potters' kiln, in which the pots were baked, and they expected Bristlepate, as his share of the work, to get the wood.

One morning the boy's mother told him to hitch up the ox and go to the forest for a load of wood. In the evening Bristlepate returned without even a stick in the cart. When his mother scolded him for not bringing the wood, he said:

"Alas, dear mother, I lay down in the shade of the tree that I was going to cut, to play my flute a few moments, and fell asleep and did not awake until the sun was setting. Please do not be angry; tomorrow I will bring the load of wood."

The next morning Bristlepate went to the forest again, but in the evening he returned with an empty cart. He told the same story, but he promised faithfully to bring two loads the next day.

The following morning, he set out early with his mind made up to keep his promise. He even left his flute at home so that he might not be tempted to play it.

When he reached the forest, he took off his coat and hat and began to chop a tree with all his might. Soon an odd-looking man, wearing a red turban, loose trousers of many colors, a close-fitting green velvet jacket, and shoes turned up at the toes, came strolling down the road. He hailed Bristlepate with the greeting of the Malays:

"We are of one blood."

"Friend," replied Bristlepate, after the manner of the tribe to which he belonged, "where did you come from and where are you going?"

"I," answered the stranger, "am from Madagascar. I am a magician. Where I am going I do not know myself."

The magician then sat down, cross-legged, upon the ground, took from his pocket a bamboo tube, and drew from it a parchment scroll with strange writing on it. As he studied the scroll Bristlepate stood by, looking on with deep interest. At length the man said:

"This book describes a charm, which I have in my possession and which your people call an anting-anting." From another pocket he then drew the charm, which looked like a small compass.

"This charm," he said, holding it so that Bristlepate could see it plainly, "will enable the wearer to make anything he wishes follow him. It was intended for but one person in this whole world, however, and that person only will it obey. I have been seeking him for many years. By my book of magic, it seems that you are like the person for whom the charm was meant. My book says the person must have a bristly head and large, black eyes, be a hauler of wood, the son of a potter, the driver of a zebu hitched to a cart, and be found in the act of chopping a tree."

By this time Bristlepate was much excited for he was sure the charm was meant for him.

"Please, sir, may I have my anting-anting," said Bristlepate, holding out his hand.

"Not yet," answered the magician. "Wait, until I take another look at my book." He then unrolled the parchment and read it again. "Here's something about the name of the person," he went on. "What is your name, young man? "

"Bristlepate!" exclaimed the youth.

"I am sorry," replied the magician as he replaced the parchment in the tube, "but the name of the person must be Wong Singsongadongon. I had hoped that I had found in you the real person, but alas, I see that I shall have to go on seeking him. Good day!"

"Wait!" called Bristlepate, as the stranger started away. "I said my name was Bristlepate, but I forgot that that was only a name the neighbors gave me. My real name is Wong Singsongadongon, and as a proof I have it tattooed here on my right arm," and he rolled up his sleeve to show the magician his arm.

"Well," said the magician, as he looked at the tattooing, "that settles it. The charm was without doubt made for you. It is worth at least two bags of gold, but as you are a poor boy, I shall trade it for the ox and cart. If you ever become wealthy, however, I shall be sure to call upon you for my share of the gold."

So Bristlepate traded off his ox and cart for the charm, and started for home on foot, while the magician got into the cart and drove away.

As might have been expected, when Bristlepate got home and told his parents about his bargain, they became very angry.

"Oh," they wailed, "you were not content to bring sorrow to us on account of your laziness, but now your foolishness has ruined us in our old days. It was all we could do to make a living with the ox to haul wood for the kiln. We shall now have to go out at night and carry the wood upon our tired backs. Woe be to us! Who would have thought our son would have been so silly as to trade an ox for a piece of tin!"

Bristlepate was greatly overcome by the wailings of his parents, and wished he had never heard of the charm, although he still believed in it. At length he asked:

"Oh, father, oh, mother, what would make you both happy once more?"

"Foolish one," they replied, "nothing less than a mountain of wood near the potter's kiln."

"Then," said Bristlepate, trying to comfort them, "if that is all, you shall be happy by tomorrow night."

"Just another one of your promises," they replied. "Today

you were to bring us two loads of wood, but you came back without ox, cart, or wood."

The next morning, long before sunrise, Bristlepate jumped out of bed, prepared his own breakfast, tied up a lunch, and set out for the hills. By noon he had climbed nearly to the top of a high mountain. He sat down beneath a great mahogany tree to rest.

"I shall now see if my anting-anting can do as the magician promised," said Bristlepate.

Rising, he walked away from the tree, under which he had been resting, and said, " Oh, tree, follow me, follow me!" The great tree began to move to and fro as if trying to pull itself out of the ground. In a moment, out it came, bringing up a great quantity of earth and rocks with it, and leaving an immense hole. Then Bristlepate started down the mountain, with the tree walking close behind him, using its strong roots as legs.

Late in the evening he came to the house of a cabinetmaker, at the side of the road, where he stopped for a drink. When the cabinetmaker saw the tree, he said:

"That's a fine mahogany tree you have, Bristlepate; what in the world are you going to do with it?"

"Chop it up for the kiln," Bristlepate replied.

"I can save you a lot of work," said the man, "I'll trade you a whole mountain of wood, already sawed into chunks, for that tree."

"Let me see this wood pile of yours," said Bristlepate.

The cabinetmaker then led Bristlepate to the back of his shop and pointed out a great pile of wood, made up of slabs, knots, and gnarled limbs, all of which he had been discarding for years. Bristlepate eagerly traded his tree for the wood, and stepping out to the road, he commanded the pile to follow him. Immediately the big wood pile began to move. Slowly it slid over the fence and along after him.

It was late when Bristlepate reached home. Going to a spot in back of the house where the kiln stood, he bade the wood stop there, and it at once settled down into a great pile covering half the yard, and higher than the tallest tree.

Bristlepate then slipped into bed and fell happily asleep. When he awoke late the next morning he heard his mother singing and his father laughing over the mountain of wood near their potter's kiln.

The next day, the boy noticed that his mother seemed sad, again.

"What is it, mother?" he asked, "you look so sorrowful and careworn. Is there anything that I can do to make you happy?"

"I was just thinking," replied the tired woman, "how I would like to have a cow. You know I was born in the country and my people always kept cows, pigs, and goats—and a big flock of ducks."

"You shall have a cow, mother, if I can get one," replied Bristlepate.

"Thank you, son," she replied. "You are a good boy."

Soon after Bristlepate set out for the mountains again. He went on and on until he came to a wild country where nobody lived. There he saw a pretty red cow with a little brindle calf at her side.

"Follow me, cow, follow me!" he shouted. Immediately the cow tossed her head into the air, looked about a moment, then trotted toward him, with the calf at her side. The boy now started down the mountain, with the cow and calf following at his heels.

On the way down he saw a goat with two kids grazing. He called to them to follow him, and they at once fell into line behind the cow and calf. Next he saw a pig with twelve little pigs.

"Pig, follow me!" he shouted. The pig and her little ones fell in behind the goat and her kids. At the foot of the mountain there was a lovely lake in which a flock of wild ducks were swimming.

"Follow me!" he called to them and the ducks rose from the water, then fell into a long line behind the pig and the twelve little pigs.

It was already night when the procession reached the potter's home. The animals lay down in the yard, the ducks settled under a shed, Bristlepate slipped away to bed, and all slept.

The next morning when Bristlepate's mother saw the animals and ducks, she was happier than she had been since she was a little girl. She ran to her son and cried out in great joy:

"Oh, son, I once thought you were a lazy lad, but now I know I was mistaken. My son is not only a hard worker, but he is wise. Son, this day you have brought great happiness to your parents."

Bristlepate by this time was eager to set out to seek his own fortune and to test his charm further. As he had helped to make his father and mother comfortable and happy they were willing that he should go out into the world.

So one morning he left home with his charm in his pocket and his flute in his hand. He hoped to become a musician, so he made his way to the city where the king lived, hoping some day that he might be flute player at the court.

Now the king had a very beautiful daughter, named Poonay, which means "pretty dove." Poonay, although she had everything money could buy to make her happy, she always seemed quite sad. She had never been known to laugh.

The king had become so concerned about this that he had published a decree that whoever could make the princess laugh, to that one would he give her in marriage. Many princes had tried, but, so far, all had failed.

When Bristlepate arrived in the king's city, he heard about the beautiful princess and the promise the king had made. He thought of his charm, and he wondered if it could be of service and help him make the princess happy.

He set out for the palace one day, hoping he might catch a glimpse of Poonay. He found a little gate that opened into the palace gardens quite unguarded, and through it he went. After wandering about awhile, admiring its beauty, he seated himself, took out his flute and began to play.

Suddenly he heard a voice say, "Oh, what beautiful music!" He looked up and there stood the princess. How beautiful she was, and oh, how sad!

Bristlepate could hardly speak, but he bowed low before Poonay, and said, " I am glad my music pleases you!"

"Oh, play again," said the princess, and Bristlepate played again.

" I would do anything to please you! " said Bristlepate.

"Oh, would you? " said the princess. "Then I wish you would come here every day and play to me! Your music is so lovely." Bristlepate gladly promised. Every day he went into the palace garden through the little gate and played for the princess.

One day the princess told him why she was sad. She was very lonely, she said. Because she was a princess, she had never been allowed to play with other children when she was little, and now that she was grown she had no friends, though plenty of suitors had come who wished to marry her.

"Oh," said the princess, "if I only had a pet of some kind I would not be so lonely. I wish I could have a kitten, but my father does not like cats."

Bristlepate declared he would find her a kitten if he had to bring all the cats in town to the garden for her to choose from. So it was agreed that the next day he was to bring Poonay a kitten.

The next morning Bristlepate, with the charm about his neck, went through many streets of the city, calling out to the cats to follow him. In a short time hundreds of cats had collected around him. There were all sorts of cats, large and small, thin and fat, and quite a number of kittens. Such a spectacle as they made following Bristlepate, purring, spitting, mewing, scratching, clawing!

It was not long before Bristlepate had a crowd of people following him as well. The princess was in the garden, waiting.

When she saw Bristlepate with his collection of cats and crowds of people pushing and jostling each other, she was so amused at the funny sight that she laughed aloud.

When the people heard Poonay laugh, they cheered and cheered. The king, hearing all the noise, came out to see the cause of it. He was met by cheers and shouts.

"Our princess has laughed! Here is the man for her to marry! He has made Princess Poonay laugh!"

When the king found out that Bristlepate was only the son of a, potter, a maker of clay pots, he would not allow the princess to marry him, even though the princess was willing. He ordered Poonay into the palace and Bristlepate out of the garden. Then Bristlepate who had fallen deeply in love with the princess said to the king, "Follow—follow me!" and the king had to follow.

Bristlepate led the king over fields and meadows, hill and dale, till the poor king was ready to promise anything if he were only allowed to return to the palace and rest his tired feet and aching bones.

So when the king agreed that Bristlepate might marry the princess, Bristlepate led him back to the palace but when the king was safely inside the palace, he refused to allow the princess to marry the potter's son, because he was poor.

Now Bristlepate had heard of a gold mine outside of the city that had not been worked for many years. Away he went to the mine with his charm, and standing at the opening of the mine, he said, "If there be gold here, follow me!"

There was a rumbling in the earth, and then gold began to come out of the depths of the mine and to collect in great heaps at Bristlepate's feet. As Bristlepate started down the mountain with the gold following him, he met the magician seated in the old cart and driving the ox.

"Oh!" said the magician, as he looked at Bristlepate and then at the gold, "I see you are now able to pay me my two bags of gold for the charm."

"That I am," said Bristlepate, and he filled two bags with gold for the magician. Each then went on his way.

When the king saw Bristlepate's gold he gave his consent to the wedding, and amid great rejoicing the princess and Bristlepate were married.

It is said that ever after, by the aid of his charm perhaps, Bristlepate could always make the princess laugh.

THE LAZY HUSBANDS

Once upon a time there was a little old toothless fellow called Bungy. He was so very lazy that it was all his washerwoman wife could do to make him go after the clothes for her to wash. She never asked him to deliver them, because she knew he would keep part of the money to buy tobacco.

One day Bungy's wife said to him, "Bungy, you are the laziest husband that ever lived on this earth."

"Oh, wife," said he, "I know I am lazy, but I am not the laziest husband in all the world by any means. I even know of one in this town that is lazier than I."

"Just show him to me," replied the woman, "and I shall never again call you lazy. Nay, I shall tell all the neighbors what an industrious man you are."

"That I shall gladly," said Bungy. "Just come down to the end of the street with me."

"I do not believe you," said his wife, "but as I have to go that way to deliver a bundle of clothes, I shall go with you."

So, she and Bungy walked down the street. Soon they came to a little shop with low, wooden shutters, and a long, narrow counter outside. The shutters were partly closed, showing the huge, bare feet of the shopkeeper sticking out, with his heels resting on the edge of the counter. Leaning against the counter was a coarse palm-leaf broom like those used for sweeping yards.

Above the shutters hung a sign, which read:

FOOD AND DRINK FOR SALE
Please do not wake me unless you wish to buy at least a dollar's worth. If you must wake me, use the broom to tickle the soles of my feet.

A. GOOTAD, Prop.

"Well, here he is," said Bungy, pointing to the feet.

Mrs. Bungy, who was a very large woman, picked up the broom and jabbed the stiff brush into the broad soles of the man's feet. The owner of the feet at once sprang up with more quickness than he had shown for many a day. He opened the shutters and stuck out his head.

"What do you want?" he demanded, trying to rub both feet at the same time.

"Give us two cents' worth of garlic," said Bungy with a grin.

"Get away from here!" cried the shopkeeper. "You're the same fellow that woke me up yesterday to buy three cents' worth of tobacco. I suppose you will be around again tomorrow to spend a penny on something. Oh, my poor feet! I've a notion to give you the worst beating you ever had in your life."

Just then he saw Bungy's wife, who stood nearby with clenched fists. The shopkeeper backed into the building, and was closing the shutters, when his own wife appeared from the market place where she had been selling dried fish.

"Customers," said she, " I shall be glad to wait upon you, no matter how little you wish to buy. That husband of mine is the laziest mortal that ever lived."

"I am indeed very sorry for you," said Mrs. Bungy. "My husband is industrious, and I do not know what I would do if he were lazy like yours."

Now this was really the first time in all his married life that Bungy had ever heard his wife say that he was industrious. He was so delighted that he turned a couple of handsprings, then grabbed the bundle of clothes, and ran with it to the owner. While the women were still talking, he returned with the money he had collected and gave it all to his wife.

"You should indeed be proud of him," said Mrs. Gootad.

"I am," said Mrs. Bungy. Bungy gave another flip.

"Oh," sobbed Mrs. Gootad, "I wish I had a husband like yours, but I married the laziest man in the whole world. He eats so much, too, that it is all I can do to support him."

"Mine is a small eater," said Mrs. Bungy.

Little Bungy turned more handsprings.

All this time Gootad had been sitting on the counter listening to the women talk. At length he said to his wife:

"I am tired of that word *lazy*. I wish it were not in the language. I know that I am lazy, but I am not as lazy as the fellow who lives over the hill on the banks of the creek."

"If you will show me a man lazier than you are," said his wife, "I shall never call you lazy again. Nay, I shall even tell all the neighbors what an industrious husband I have."

"Come," said Gootad, getting up from the counter, "but I wish these people to go along as witnesses. I am afraid you will not keep your word if we go alone."

So the two couples set out to find the man of whom Gootad had spoken. In an hour or so they had crossed the hill and had come to a little stream, whose clear water trickled between narrow banks lined with banana trees. Underneath the trees grew a thick matting of yam and peanut vines.

"Well, here he is," said Gootad, pointing to a man sleeping in a rattan hammock swung under the trees, near the edge of the stream.

Over the hammock, and within the sleeper's reach, were several large clusters of bananas in all stages of growth, from the tiniest green one to the large, mellow kind.

Gootad shook the sleeper, who woke up with a scowl, but when he saw who it was that had awakened him, he changed his expression and said

"Gootad, I was just dreaming of a pleasant smoke. Give me a cigar, please."

Gootad took a large black cigar from his pocket and handed it to the man, who at once put it into his mouth and began to puff away after Gootad had lighted it for him.

"Who are these people you have brought along?" drawled the fellow.

"They are some friends of mine who would like to hear your story," replied Gootad.

"Tell them to go away and leave me alone," said the hammock man. "It always makes me tired to tell my story."

"Come," said Gootad, "I shall give you a dozen cigars like the one you have in your mouth if you will tell it."

"Will you throw in enough matches to light the cigars?" the man asked.

"I will," said Gootad.

"Well, it is this way," began the hammock dweller in drawling tones. "My wife used to scold me from morning till night on account of my laziness. I put up with this state of affairs for twenty years. Then one day I said, ' I will not stand this any longer. ' So I came here and planted these banana trees, with yams and peanuts underneath them. When the trees began to bear I swung this hammock in the shade, and have been in it ever since, except for two or three times when I had to go out and beg a little smoking tobacco. When I want anything to eat all I do is to reach up and pull off a banana. In case I wish a change of diet, I put down a foot and dig out a yam or a few peanuts with my toes. If I want a drink I take this long, hollow reed here and draw the water from the cool spring you see under the head of my hammock. I hope to start a patch of tobacco some of these days, and when it is grown I'll get me a pipe, something to light it with, and put a hook on the end of my drinking reed. With the hook I can reach out and pull off the tobacco leaves; thus my peace and happiness will be complete. You see, Gootad, it is my ambition to live so that I shall never, for any reason, have to leave my hammock. I've heard of places where it was cold a part of the year and where people had to plant their crops every few months, but I'm very thankful I do not live in such a country. If you men wish to try my experiment there is plenty of room farther up the creek."

"Dear husbands, let's go home," said the women at the end of the hammock-dweller's story.

Whether because of the promises they had made, or a secret fear that their husbands might be tempted to live as the hammock dweller lived, the two women for ever afterwards kept their word. The queer thing about it is that Bungy and Gootad actually became industrious.

In less than a year little Bungy was elected mayor. His wife then gave up washing and lived a life of ease. Things likewise turned out well with Gootad. He worked so hard that he became rich and kept many servants. Whenever he drove out in his fine carriage for an airing, the people said:

"There goes the industrious one."

THE PROUD COOK OF MANILA

Few years before the Spaniards came to the country now known as the Philippines, there ruled in the city of May-nilad (the ancient name for Manila) a powerful old Malay chieftain, or petty king, by the name of Matanda. In those days, rich merchants from China came to May-nilad every few weeks in their great sailing junks to trade with the islanders. One time a merchant asked Matanda if he would like the king of China, to send him a fine present. After thinking the matter over, Matanda said he would be pleased if the great king would send him a good cook. The merchant was a little surprised at what Matanda had asked for, because he had expected the chief to ask for something of great value. Still, he promised to bring one of the best cooks that could be found in all China upon his next trip.

So, when the merchant returned, he brought the cook. His name was Pflung-Chow-High, but as that was too long a name for Matanda to say when ordering his meals, he called the new cook "Chow"

Now Chow was a mighty fine cook, but he was very proud. He wore a purple silk gown, felt shoes, a tight-fitting skullcap surmounted with a rosette, and a long braid of hair, or a queue, that hung down his back almost to his heels.

Whenever he went to market to buy things for the king's table, or simply out for an airing, he took along a whole troop of servants to wait upon him. From the way he dressed, gave orders, and strutted about, one who did not know him would have thought that he was a prime minister at least.

The old king commanded Chow never to turn anyone who was hungry from his door; also each evening to place some choice bits of food beneath a tall palm tree back of the kitchen, as an offering to the earth people. "We believe," said the king, "that the earth people are our forefathers, and for that reason we honor them. Remember this, too, Chow," cautioned the king, "although the earth people live in the ground, they are very clean, and nothing offends them so much as for careless people to throw anything unclean upon it. The little creatures cannot often be seen, but we feel they are about us in great numbers. For this reason, we have a custom of giving a warning before casting out anything that might soil them. Remember, then, whenever you have need to do anything of the kind, to warn the earth people in these words: "Worthy forefathers, look out!"

"Ah," said the proud cook to himself, after he had left the king's presence, "if I am kind to the poor there will always be a lot of them around begging for food, and that will mean more work, so I shall not go to the trouble of feeding them. Then, as to these earth people: they may be Matanda's forefathers, but they are not mine. No, I shall certainly not waste any breath in warning them to get out of my way. They must look out for themselves, or take the consequences."

Not long afterward a poor old man came to the king's kitchen and asked for something to eat. Although the man was plainly weary as well as hungry, Chow turned him away without so much as giving him a morsel of cold boiled rice.

Likewise he paid no attention to what the king had said about making food offerings to the earth people; neither did he warn them before he threw things upon the ground. He was a master of his art, though, and not only prepared the home dishes in a manner that greatly pleased the king, but he brought in many new ones that had caused the great emperor of China to smack his lips. On account of his skill, his fame soon spread far and wide, so that the chief men of the island kingdom were only too glad to get a chance to eat of his cooking.

Once Matanda invited all the chief men of the kingdom to a feast. The food was placed upon a long, low table in the middle of the great dining hall. When all the guests had squatted around the table, Chow brought in a soup pot as big as a tub. While the king was telling his company of the fine soup they were about to taste, the cook raised the lid in order to dip out the contents. To the amazement of all present, he had no sooner lifted the cover than out sprang a dozen or more great, green frogs!

"Ho!" exclaimed the king in a rage, as the animals hopped about on the table, blinking their queer, bright eyes, "what kind of cold Chinese stew is this you are serving us? How is it that when I ask for my favorite soup, you upset our stomachs with a pot of green toads? Out of here!" he roared, without giving Chow a chance to say a word. "From now on you shall be the feeder of my pigs!"

Thus, by a word, the once proud feeder of kings became a poor feeder of swine. He had to lay aside his fine clothing for an old ragged shirt, a squash helmet, and a pair of wide, short trousers made of coarse hemp fiber.

Every morning, amidst the jeers of those who had been his servants, he collected the scraps from the royal kitchen into a couple of tall, bulging jars. Then he slung each of the jars to the end of a long, springy pole, threw the pole over his shoulders, and jog-trotted with the heavy load to the edge of the Pasig river. Here he placed the vessels in a boat and paddled up stream several miles to Matanda's pig ranch.

Now it was bad enough for the Chinaman to have to endure the taunts of kitchen servants, but to make things worse, the boys who tended the swine took a delight in making fun of him. Sometimes when they saw him coming they would say, "Here comes Uncle," and when he went away in his wide trousers, "There goes Auntie."

Even the animals he fed seemed to have no respect for him. Once when he was trudging from the boat with the heavy jars, the greedy creatures would not wait for him to pour their food into the trough. Instead, they ran between his legs and threw him upon his back. They then trampled upon him, squealed in his ears, scratched his shins with their sharp tusks, and poked him in the ribs with the tough ends of their snouts, as they rolled him about and fought over the spilled food.

Chow, with very good reason, felt that all his bad luck came from the earth people, and, after this terrible experience, he promised himself to pay them back for the disgrace they had brought upon him. From this time on he kept a sharp lookout for earth people, waiting and longing for a chance to repay the terrible injury which he felt they had inflicted on him.

To his joy before long his chance came. Early one morning as he was paddling up the river with his cargo, he espied several strange little people sitting upon a soft, grassy spot on the bank. They sat in a circle, and from the way they tossed their arms, wagged their jaws, and nodded their heads, they seemed to be discussing something of great importance.

"Oho!" said Chow, under his breath, "there are the little imps—planning some more mischief for me no doubt." He tied up his boat, took one of the jars in his arms, and stole up to where the dwarfish creatures had gathered. Lifting the vessel high above his head, he dashed the contents over the little beings at his feet, and called out, "There, unworthy forefathers, I hope I have given you a pleasant bath!"

From under the great jar came splashy sounds, mingled with gurglings, and angry shouts. The kettle was turned upright in a minute or two, but the earth people were nowhere to be seen. Only a dirty pool remained where they had been holding their meeting a short time before.

Chow chuckled to himself. He felt that he had got even with his enemies but he was not satisfied with what he had done, and as he kept on his way up the river, he planned how he could injure them further.

That afternoon he lay down upon his back in the shade of a small mango tree. His lying down, though, was not so much for the purpose of resting tired muscles, as it was for plotting mischief. Close to where his head lay, the pigs had scooped out a deep, funnel-like hole, by rooting for fat grubs, tender grassroots, and other tidbits of the soil. His queue fell over the edge of the funnel, and gradually unrolled itself until the end rested at the bottom.

Pretty soon he felt a tugging at his hair. He tried to get up, but the more he tried the greater the tugging. His head was gradually drawn into the opening, then his shoulders. Just as he was nearly out of sight, a couple of strong pig herders, who happened to be near, saw a pair of wiggling legs, the soles of whose feet were directed toward the sky. They ran up, grabbed hold of the legs, and tried with all their might to draw the owner of them out, but no matter how hard the fellows pulled, the upturned limbs, inch by inch, went deeper into the ground.

In a mighty struggle to free the Chinaman, the two men braced themselves, clenched their teeth, and heaved with might and main. At length they began to bring him up, but just as they had got his knees upon a level with the rim of the funnel, a thing happened that ended all their helpfulness. Chow's shoes slipped off, and this caused both his friends to tumble over backwards, each with a shoe in his hands. Before they could rise, Chow had disappeared, soul and body, into the earth.

The young men hurried away to report Chow's disappearance to Matanda. At the close of their story the king merely scratched his head, plucked a bristle from his eyebrows, and asked the boys why they hadn't brought the jars home.

After telling their news, the young men went back to their work of tending the pigs. They looked for the jars, which they had left near the spot where the Chinaman had disappeared. The jars as well as the carrying pole were gone, although close to the opening lay the shoes and the squash helmet. Chow's clothes were given to his successor and Matanda took some money from the two pig herders' wages to pay for new jars. He did this, not because he was mean or angry, but to teach all his careless servants a lesson.

Chow's going away caused no worry whatever, although it did cause everyone to wonder. Hardly anyone would believe that he had been swallowed up by the earth. Such a thing was possible, they said, only in case of an earthquake, but there had been no earthquake for a long time.

Many thought the Chinaman had gotten away to his native land on a boat belonging to his countrymen. Others that he had run off to the mountains and taken up with a tribe of dog eaters (*The Igorots*); and there were even a few stubborn old farmers, living near by, who declared that he must have been killed by the swineherds and thrown into the Pasig river.

Where was Chow?

The tiny earth folk, of course, as the pig herders knew, as Matanda knew, and as everybody else ought to have known, could tell what had become of Chow.

When his queue fell into the hole the elves came up from below and tied a long rope to the end of it. Then hundreds of them, pulling on the rope, drew their enemy into a dark passageway that led directly to their country in the hollow of the earth. At the end of this passageway they bound him, hand and foot, then dragged him down a long slope until they came to a huge, bronze door that opened into a region far lighter than if the sun were shining into it.

After the underground pigmies had gotten their captive through the door, they buckled upon him a kind of harness, with long ropes fastened here and there to a rawhide band that went around his middle. They now took hold of the loose ends of the ropes, and when one of their number had cut the cords that bound the prisoner's legs, they ordered him to get up.

At once he scrambled to his feet. After they had allowed him to get his balance, they marched him down a wide road, with his captors in front of him, behind him, and at his sides. Thus he was forced to go along just like a Bengal tiger who is being taken by jungle trappers to a place that buys circus animals.

However, Chow did not act like a tiger; he acted as meek as a pet kitten that is being led across the nursery floor by a wisp of pink yarn.

After several hours, Chow was brought to the capital of the underground empire. As he came near, there was great excitement, especially upon the part of the pigmy children. They came pouring out of their homes to see the captive giant.

So great was the disturbance that a company of royal guards had to be called out to clear the streets of the youngsters. The prisoner was then led before the judge, who, after he had heard all that everyone had to say, promptly sentenced him to be kept alone in prison for five years.

When you remember what Chow had done, this was really not very severe punishment, for it seems that one of the earth men upon whom he had spilled the dishwater was a prince, and another a high officer of the court. Had such a deed been done in Chow's own country, he would have been led out at once to have his head cut off.

After Chow had been locked up for something like three years, the earth king decided to give a feast to all the lords and ladies of his court. In order to have it ready on time, he had to employ all the cooks in the country; and yet there were not enough to do the work. Then someone remembered Chow, shut up in his lonely prison, and he was ordered out to help with the rougher work.

Now he displayed such great skill in the finer points of his old occupation, that the cooks who feared the king's displeasure if the feast should prove a failure, soon put him in charge of everything.

When the royal banquet was over, everybody said that the food had been so plentiful, so varied, and so fine that it was the best dinner they had ever eaten. Even His Majesty, the earth king, was so well pleased with the feast that he called the chief cook before the throne in order that he might thank him but the honest chief cook told the king the truth—that Chow deserved all the praise and credit. The king sent for his old enemy.

"Chow," said he, "you have done so well in this matter that I am going to reward you. You shall be the chief of all my cooks. I will pay you double the amount that my friend, Matanda, paid you. At the end of two years come around for your wages. You may then go back a free man to the upper world."

Chow was overjoyed at this piece of good news. The time flew by so fast that he did not know when his two years were up. In fact, he stayed for nearly four years. He then went to the king and asked to be dismissed.

"You have been a most faithful and humble servant," said the king, "and have remained in my service a great deal longer than I expected. Go to my paymaster and get your wages."

The paymaster, after figuring for half an hour, asked Chow how he was going to carry his money home.

"In my pockets, sir," said Chow, a little surprised. "Your pockets will not hold such a great amount," said the paymaster, looking at his figures. "Better bring in your jars."

Chow went out to get the jars, thinking that he was to be paid off in the little bronze "cash" or coin of China.

When he came back the paymaster led him into the treasury where a great pile of gold lay heaped upon the floor.

"Help yourself," said the paymaster. " How much of this belongs to me? " asked Chow, in great wonder at the sight of so much money.

"All of it," said the official.

Without asking any more questions, Chow shoveled the gold into his jars and carried the vessels outside, one at a time. Here he fastened them to his carrying pole, and then followed a guide along the underground passageway to the surface of the earth.

"Here," said the little guide, pointing to an ancient mango tree, "is the place where you came in. Good day! and good luck."

"The little fellow must be mistaken," said Chow as he wiped the sweat from his forehead. "The tree under which I lay was only a shrub, and this one is very large and very old. It is true, the mountains are the same, and there is the river—but even the river looks different."

At first he felt like whistling for the pig herders, but upon second thought he decided not to, because he was afraid if Matanda learned that he was free, he would put him back at his old job of feeding the pigs. He sat down upon one of the money jars, and while he was wondering what to do he looked up and saw a boat coming down the river.

"Where are you going, friend?" he shouted to the boatman.

"To the river's mouth," answered the man, rowing toward the bank. "Hop in, if you are going my way."

Chow lifted his jars into the boat, and was soon traveling down the river.

"Are you a stranger in these parts?" asked the boatman.

"Not exactly," said Chow, "but I have been away for a few years, and everything has changed so much that I can scarcely recognize anything but the mountains."

"In these days things change rapidly," said the boatman.

"I see that King Matanda has moved his pig ranch," said Chow as he noticed the cultivated fields along the banks.

"Sir," said the boatman, turning around to look at his companion, "I do not know what you mean. I have never heard of a King Matanda, neither has there been a pig ranch anywhere about here since I was born. Are you sure that you know where you are and where you are going?"

"Am I not in a boat, on a river that flows from a lake in the middle of an island?" asked Chow.

"You are," said the boatman.

"Do they call this river the Pasig, the lake Bai, and the island Luzon? " asked Chow.

"They do," said the boatman.

"And is there a city called May-nilad on the left bank of this river near where it flows into the sea? " continued Chow.

"They used to call it that, I think," said the boatman, "but they changed it to Manila, even before the time of my great-grandfather."

"Well," said Chow, "take me to this city, whatever they call it, or did call it, and you shall have a good fee for your trouble."

In a little while they came in sight of a great city, with a high wall and wide moat surrounding it.

"Is this May-nilad?" asked Chow.

"It is what was," said the boatman.

"Does Matanda still rule it?" asked Chow.

"No!" said the boatman. "Didn't I tell you that I never heard of this King Matanda? Manila as well as the whole country is ruled by a Spanish governor; but I do not know the present one's name. They change governors so often that I can't keep up with them. Man," continued the boatman, somewhat out of patience with his passenger's stupidity, "have you just dropped down from above?"

"No," said Chow, "I have just come up from below."

Upon hearing these words the boatman—who was a Christian—crossed himself, for, by this time, he felt almost assured that his passenger was none other than the Evil One himself. He hastily drew his boat in to the landing, helped to lift out the jars, and then started to push away without waiting for a fee.

"Here!" said Chow, handing him a gold piece.

"Evil One, or no Evil One," said the boatman to himself, as he rowed off, "the fellow pays well."

In Manila, Chow met with many of his countrymen, but none whom he had ever seen before. Through them he learned of the coming of the Spaniards, and all the great changes they had brought about. He soon got used to the new order of things, but what greatly puzzled him was that he felt no older than he did when he went into the ground over a hundred years before. Indeed, he felt so young, looked so young, and in fact, was so young, that he sent to China for a pretty young wife.

When she came, he gave such a grand wedding feast that it was the talk of the town for a whole month. And no wonder they talked about it, because no less than fifty hogs were roasted in order to provide meat for the guests, which included such noble personages as the Spanish governor and his lady.

After the honeymoon was over, the Chinaman set up a large grocery shop near the heart of the city, and had this sign painted in large letters above the door:

CHOW, GOOD THINGS TO EAT

The rich Chinaman kept so much good food in stock that he soon had more customers than all the other Manila grocerymen put together. Before long everyone began to call all good food "chow."

In the course of time the term "chow" spread to other countries. To this day the soldiers and sailors of all nations call everything that is eatable "chow," no matter whether it be chop suey, stewed prunes, or Hungarian goulash.

MR. MONK AND THE ALLIGATOR

Far away in the jungles, a tribe of monkeys made their home near a lake. They were very happy until a great old alligator came to the lake to live. After that, every time anyone went to the lake for a drink, the hungry alligator would try to catch him, for there was nothing that he liked better than monkey meat. Almost every week he caught some poor creature in his strong jaws.

The monkeys would have moved away, but they had lived there so long that no-one could tell when they had come. There were many nuts and fruits growing about the lake, so they did not want to give up their old home. But something had to be done. Nearly every family in the tribe mourned a relative who had helped to satisfy the appetite of the old alligator.

One day the monkeys held a meeting to see what could be done to get rid of their enemy. At this meeting all the wise monkeys made long speeches about the old alligator and the great harm he had done, but when it came to suggesting a way to get rid of him, no-one had a plan to offer. As the meeting was about to break up, an old fellow who had not spoken before stood up and made a speech in a thin, squeaky voice.

"Friends," he began, "the last time I went to the other side of the mountain, I met a clever fellow there whom all the junglefolks call Mr. Monk. I believe he could tell us some way to get rid of our enemy, the alligator. It seems a pity to give up our homes just because this old fellow has come among us and lays claim to our lake, forbidding us, on pain of death, to drink of its water, because the lake belongs to him and we have no right to drink the water. The lake is not his; we were here first, as you know. We must not leave it, yet this terrible loss of life must stop! If you all agree, I say that we name a committee to visit Mr. Monk and ask him to help us."

"Good!" shouted all the monkeys together. "Why didn't someone think of that before? We've all heard how wise Mr. Monk is."

So they named a committee of three, each member of which had lost some close friend or relative in the jaws of the alligator.

Early one morning the three monkeys chosen for the committee—the old one who had made the speech, a young monkey, and a widow whose husband the alligator had caught but a few days before, set out for the other side of the mountain to see Mr. Monk.

Late in the afternoon they reached the wise monkey's home, but they found him in a bad temper. He was sick from eating unripe bananas. The wind had just blown away the large limb of the tree upon which he slept and, to make matters worse, a young chap whom he had hired to scratch his back had gone off and got married, and could not be depended upon any more.

When the chairman of the committee made known the purpose of the visit, Mr. Monk said he did not wish to be bothered with other people's troubles; he had enough of his own.

"But," said the spokesman," it was only last week that our enemy ate my poor little grandson, the joy of the whole tribe. Please, Mr. Monk, have pity and come to our aid."

"It seems to me that one of your age and experience ought to have sense enough to get rid of a stupid old alligator," said Mr. Monk. "Let this young monkey tell his tale."

The young monkey stood up and told how the alligator had eaten up his sweetheart, but he was so awkward and blubbered in such a manner that he made the grouchy monkey laugh.

"One of your age is not expected to know anything," said Mr. Monk, " although you are strong enough to tie the jaws of the alligator if someone could teach you. Let the third member be heard!"

When the widow told how her husband had been carried off in the horrible jaws, she was so overcome with grief that she nearly fainted. Even the cross Mr. Monk was touched by the young widow's story.

"For this poor widow's sake," he said, "I will agree to help you get rid of the alligator, but I will ask you to provide me with three things: first, a comfortable tree for a home; second, a supply of good ripe bananas and coconuts; third, someone to scratch my back."

"I will supply the bananas and coconuts," said the old monkey.

"I will scratch your back," said the young monkey.

"I will find you a home," said the widow.

"Very well," replied Mr. Monk, "under those conditions I promise you that your enemy will soon be where he will never eat anyone else."

Mr. Monk then went back to the lake with the members of the committee. He found the alligator sunning himself on a log in the lake. Creeping up to the edge of the water he called out:

"Hey there, Old Scaly Back, why don't you open your eyes? It is time all honest folk were awake, whether they live upon land, in the air, or in the water."

The alligator opened his eyes, at these bold words, and seeing a monkey on the shore, dived into the water and began to swim toward him as fast as he could. Just before the alligator reached the bank, Mr. Monk leaped into a tree nearby and climbed to the top of it where the young monkey sat holding a large coconut in his hands.

The alligator stood under the tree and opened his big jaws so wide that one could see way down his throat.

"Look," he said to Mr. Monk. "Here's the road that many a monkey has traveled, and it will not be long before you will travel it, too. There's a monkey at the end of the road now," he said, pointing to his stomach with one of his paws.

Mr. Monk stretched out his neck and looked down into the great mouth of the alligator.

"Oh, I can see the poor fellow's nose!" he said. "A little wider, please, so that I may see his head." The alligator opened his mouth wider. "Oh, I can see the poor fellow's head!" said the monkey. "A little wider, please, so that I may see his body." The alligator opened his wider.

"Oh, I can see the poor fellow's body!" said the monkey. "A little wider, please, so that I may see his tail."

The alligator opened his mouth so wide that it nearly dislocated his jaws.

"Oh, I can see the poor fellow's tail!" said Mr. Monk. Just as he uttered the word "tail" he threw the coconut into the alligator's mouth. Down went the coconut into the alligator's throat. The old alligator choked, snorted, and coughed in an effort to get the nut out of his throat, but try as he might, he could not dislodge it.

When the monkeys saw the alligator choking and coughing on the ground with the coconut in his throat, they came down from the trees, and danced, chattered, and laughed in great glee.

The old alligator rolled over and over until he came to the edge of the lake, where he dived into the water and disappeared; but all night he could be heard coughing and choking, trying to get the coconut out of his throat.

Early in the morning, Mr. Monk went down to the edge of the lake. He found the alligator asleep on a log, but the coconut was no longer in his mouth. He had gotten rid of it in some way.

"Ah!" said Mr. Monk to himself, "I see I shall have to try some other means."

Going to the forest Mr. Monk climbed up a bush in which hung a large, round hornet's nest. With a ball of mud he stopped up the opening in the nest. He then broke off the nest, placed it under his arm and carried it to the lake. Just as he came to the edge of the water the alligator opened his eyes. The monkey sat down quietly upon a tuft of grass and said aloud as if he were talking to someone nearby:

"This is surely a fine watermelon. If there is anything that I like better than a coconut it is a watermelon."

The alligator slipped off the log and swam toward the bank. "Oh," he said to himself, "what a fine breakfast is waiting for me, monkey and watermelon!"

Just as he was about to seize him, Mr. Monk gave a mighty leap, and ran with the hornet's nest under his arm toward the tree. Close at his heels came the alligator, his great jaws wide apart. As the monkey sprang into the tree he dropped the nest into the alligator's open jaws. Snap! Went the strong jaws on the nest, for the silly old alligator was sure it was a watermelon.

"Buzz, buzz," said the hornets. In a moment they were sticking their sharp stingers into the alligator's tongue, eyes, nose, and the sides of his big, red throat. This made the alligator cough and choke, and roll over and over.

Back to the lake he crawled with the whole swarm of hornets clinging about his head, and driving their stingers into every soft spot they could find in his scaly old hide. Into the lake he rolled, and was not seen again that day.

That evening Mr. Monk chose several strong monkeys to follow him to the side of a rocky hill, where he selected an odd-shaped rock that looked very much like a monkey.

"Take this stone," he said to the young monkeys, "to the edge of the lake and hide it behind the clump of rushes that grow upon the steep bank."

The young monkeys carried the stone to the lake and set it up behind the rushes as Mr. Monk had told them.

Next morning Mr. Monk went to the lake. The alligator was asleep on the log—but what a condition he was in! His eyes were swollen, his tongue was sticking out of his mouth, and his lips turned wrong side out. Mr. Monk could hardly keep from laughing out loud when he saw him. The hornets had done their work well.

Putting his paws into the water, the monkey brought up a lot of slippery mud. With this he smeared the stone monkey all over. He then bent down the rushes and hid himself in them. He now began to laugh,

"Ho, ho, ho! What a silly thing it was to think a hornet's nest was a watermelon!"

The alligator tried to open his eyes, but they were so swollen that he was able to see only a little from the corners of them. Into the water he slid and swam toward the bank. On he came while Mr. Monk still laughed.

Just as wise Mr. Monk hoped, his sight was so bad this morning that he mistook the stone monkey for a real monkey, and opened his great mouth as wide as he could in order to be sure to get him. Mr. Monk who stood behind the stone slyly tipped it over into the big mouth. Down it slipped, right into his stomach and down, down went the cruel old alligator to the very bottom of the lake, and he has never been able to come to the top again, on account of the heavy stone in his stomach.

That very evening so it is said—Mr. Monk and the widow got married, and not only they, but all the rest of the monkeys lived in peace and happiness ever afterwards.